WHEN MONSTERS RISE

THE MONSTERS AMONG US BOOK 4

DEBBIE CASSIDY

CONTENTS

CHAPTER 1

RUE

It wasn't until I was halfway done with my glass of water that I sensed the thing in the kitchenette with me. Gooseflesh broke out up my arms, and my nape tightened as the hairs stood to attention.

But this wasn't the first time I'd sensed the presence, so I continued to sip my water, acutely aware of the shadow in the corner of the room.

It stood perfectly still, blending into the pockets of darkness around it, but my primal instincts recognized it as *other*.

As not belonging.

"I know you're there." My voice was a whisper

when I wanted it to be strong and sure. "Who are you? What do you want?"

The shadow shifted, and my stomach clenched in apprehension.

"Who are you talking to?" Bastian padded into the room, and the presence dissipated. He wrapped his arms around me from behind and rested his chin on my head. "Hey?"

"The shadow."

"The ghost?"

"It was here. I know Sarq said that Dad moved on, but what if..." I didn't want to finish the sentence. To contemplate that my father could be stuck here.

Bastian hugged me tighter. "This ghost could be anyone. This place...the death...You're more receptive than most, and it's probably just...lonely."

Which was exactly what Shem had said too, after he'd torn the room apart searching for the ghost as if it was a spider he could squish.

"Come back to bed," Bastian said.

I set my glass down and turned in his arms. "Which bed?"

His chest rumbled in a chuckle. "As much as I'd like to steal you away, Shem has his limits."

I lifted my chin, offering him my lips. "Communal bed it is then."

He pressed his lips to mine briefly, sighing softly as he pulled away. "Sharing isn't easy."

I pushed up on my toes and kissed him again. "Tomorrow night."

"Tomorrow."

Over the past seven days, we'd alternated where I slept. One night with Bastian, the other with Shem, and then a night with everyone in the room. Tomorrow was my solo time with Bastian.

As Bastian led me out of the room, I couldn't help but glance back at the spot between the counter and the fridge where my ghostly stalker had stood moments ago.

The shadows were now innocuous and flat.

Whatever had been in this room with me was gone.

SHEM WAS awake when I returned to our room, the others fast asleep on the floor around our mattress. It had been easier to remove the bedframe from the room instead of moving it around every other day.

Sarq snored softly, but Tumiel and Zaq slept soundlessly. Bastian hovered by the door as I climbed over the watchers' sleeping bodies to the main bed. Shem's eye whites gleamed where they caught the light trickling in from the hallway, giving him an almost eerie look.

Heck, if I wasn't so familiar with him, I'd have been

spooked. But the crimson-skinned watcher, with his feral features and talon-tipped horns, was nothing less than beauty to me now. I loved the sensation of his silken chestnut hair running through my fingers and the scrape of his fangs against my throat. His body was familiar. It was mine, just as Bastian's was, and I'd accepted there was no shame in wanting...in needing them both.

Shem held out his hand, and I took it, allowing him to brace me as I lowered myself onto the mattress beside him, but his attention remained on the door, on Bastian, who continued to watch us.

"You want to sleep with us?" Shem asked finally.

I froze in surprise. Had he just—

"We can make space," Shem continued.

Bastian's shoulders dropped slightly. "Not tonight. But maybe next time."

My gaze flew to his, and he offered me a small smile before retreating and closing the door.

"You don't want him here?" Shem asked softly.

"It's not that. I just...I didn't think *you'd* want him here."

"Maybe a week ago, I would have minded, but now...things have changed."

"You like him."

"He's a good man. Deserving. I wouldn't share you otherwise."

"You make it sound like it's all up to you."

He gripped my neck firmly and forced my head up so he could scan my face. "You can pretend otherwise, Rue, but you know you belong to me. That this"—he cupped my pussy, and my breath hitched—"belongs to me."

"Shem..." My voice trembled. "We're not alone."

"You think I care?"

No, I didn't suppose he did but, "I do. I care."

"I can wait." He turned my head away from him and ran his thick, long tongue up my neck. My core clenched, and a soft whimper of need escaped from my lips. "Question is, can you?" He pressed down on my pussy, and my hips rose to meet his palm. Fuck, I wanted him to touch me. I needed him to. His lips coasted against my ear, warm breath teasing the shell. "How quiet can you be?" He stroked me through my panties, purring when he felt how wet I was. "Can you be quiet, little human?" His breathless tone had me aching.

Dammit, this was wrong. I shouldn't. "Yes. I can be quiet."

"Will you hold the door closed and keep the power at bay?"

"Yes."

I was getting better at keeping the door between me and the Morningstar power closed.

He slipped his hand into my panties, and I held my breath, trembling with anticipation as he dipped

me with wet heat. He fucked me with his fingers for
achingly long minutes, bringing me closer and closer
to the edge. Tears burned my eyes as I held back the
cries clawing at the inside of my throat.

It took everything I had not to make a sound, not to
allow the channel to the Morningstar power to open.

Shem's chest heaved, his eyes dark and all-encompassing as they drank me in, bringing me close to
release, only to deny me.

"Dammit." I whisper-growled the word, and he
kissed me hard on the mouth, slipping his hand free.
The next few moments were an exercise in dexterity as
he helped me take off my pants before settling between
my thighs. This felt good. This...the ridges of his cock,
the girth, the hardness.

He rubbed himself against me, coating himself in
my juices, his breath ragged and uneven as he held
back from coming undone.

I gripped his hips, then his ass, digging my nails in
while opening wider for him.

Please.

Please.

Oh please.

He entered me slowly, filling the emptiness with his essence. The Morningstar power pressed at my senses, surging and desperate to be free. But I pushed it back, pressing my will against the door and abandoning my body to Shem.

He moved slow and easy, long strokes that deepened. He kissed me with leisurely exploration, his tongue teasing mine, his teeth grazing my lips while his fingers sank into my hair, clenching and unclenching like a heartbeat. My heart felt too large for my chest, my breath twisted and trapped in my lungs because this wasn't fucking. Not anymore...

I'd told him that I wasn't playing games. That my heart was involved, and he'd admitted the same, but this...

This was making love.

We were making love.

My heart was more than *involved*. It was invested.

I loved Shem.

WE DIDN'T SPEAK AFTERWARDS, but he held me—his chest to my back, his arm a welcome weight around my waist—caging me to his body. Our hearts beat in tandem, and after a while, his breathing slowed and his arm grew heavier, but for me, sleep was a long time coming as doubts moved in.

I'd loved Jamie and lost him. I loved Bastian, but if I didn't find a way to cure the damage the serum had done to his body, I'd lose him too. And now Shem... What would happen if we succeeded in putting the Morningstar back together? The monsters would be expelled back to Gehenna, but what about the celestials? Shem had said they'd be free to return home, but everything I'd seen and learned led me to believe that the Dominions didn't want to go to heaven. That they'd orchestrated the fall and wanted this world. We'd rid ourselves of one type of monster, only to be left with another. We'd have to *make* them leave, which meant war and death and...

I might lose Shem. I might lose Bastian, Bee and the watchers, and everyone I cared about.

My chest ached.

Breathe. Just...

One step at a time, Rue.

But the stakes seemed suddenly much higher.

As I finally drifted off to sleep, something shifted in the shadows by the door. But the stab of alarm was buried beneath a wave of exhaustion. I caught the impression of two orange eyes glowing in the dark just before sleep dragged me under.

CHAPTER 2

"The ghost had orange eyes?" Bee frowned. "That can't be normal."

"I know. I need to speak to Shem about it, but he and the watchers were gone when I woke. Bastian too."

I'd woken alone in a cocoon of blankets and immediately been assaulted by the memory of the orange eyes. There was something in our haven, and yes, it hadn't tried to attack me or anyone else, but that didn't mean it wouldn't.

We needed to understand what we were dealing with here.

"I saw Shem with Michael a little while ago," Bee said, "and Bastian is doing a security check with Tumiel." Her cheeks grew pink when she said the watcher's name.

I arched a brow. "You've been spending a lot of time with Tumiel the past few days. Anything you want to tell me?"

She dropped her gaze, picking at a cracked spot on the plastic table. "There's nothing to tell. He's nice, and he makes me feel...safe." She exhaled and shook her head. "I don't know, Rue. I mean, Ryan is dead, and I...How can I be feeling this way about someone else?"

"Because life is short. Because we could die tomorrow, and we need to take every moment of happiness we can and hold it close. Cherish it. Ryan would want you to be happy. Looked after. Safe. Don't deny yourself that."

"Even if I did decide to get to know Tumiel more, I'm bonded to Michael."

"That doesn't mean anything. He did that to save your life. He's not going to hold you to it."

Her smile was weary. "Maybe when this is all over... When we're safe and the monsters and power-hungry celestials are gone..."

I reached across the table and took her hand. "Not maybe. Definitely."

"Can I join you?" Sissy asked, holding up her breakfast tray.

"Of course, you can." Bee beamed at her. "How were morning classes?"

"Good. We did some reading today."

"Rue? You got a minute?" Mira called from across the dining hall.

I excused myself and hurried to join the woman who kept this place ticking. No one had officially said it, but it was obvious that Mira oversaw the humans. She was in charge of the food and supplies, and the fact that she was also dating one of the elite watchers made her position here unquestionable. But right now, she looked more than a little upset.

Mira didn't get annoyed easily. "What's up?"

She jerked her head toward the kitchens, a space where only she and a couple of other people were allowed. I followed her inside. With the breakfast rush over, the place was empty.

She closed the door and stood hands on hips. "I hate to say it, and I've held off because I wanted to be sure, but we got us a thief."

"What?"

"Started a week ago. At least, that's when I noticed supplies were missing."

"Shit. Are you sure?"

She fixed her dark eyes on me. "Positive. Now the only thing that's changed in the last week is you bringing the celestial and your friend back here, and as far as I'm aware, celestials don't need food."

"Wait a second, if you think that Bee—"

"I don't." She sighed. "I checked her quarters. But something *has* changed." She chewed on her cheeks.

"The storeroom is locked. I'm the only one with a key, so unless *I've* been stealing food in my sleep, then someone somehow is managing to get into a locked room."

"Vents?"

"None big enough for a person."

But a spider...No, Kabiel wouldn't use the vents to steal food, and if any of the other devolved watchers were finding their way into the mall via the vents, then they wouldn't be hitting the storeroom. The kind of food they wanted wasn't kept there. No, this wasn't a devolved watcher job.

"I heard you talking about some ghost?" Mira said. "I asked Zaq, and he told me about this shadow you've been seeing?"

"You think the *ghost* took the food?"

"I think maybe we're not dealing with a ghost at all."

Yeah, I was beginning to suspect the same. "I think you're right. I saw it last night. It has orange eyes."

"Maybe you brought something back with you," she said. "Goodness knows there are things out there that we have no grasp on."

"I'll speak to Shem about it. We will figure this out." And we had more than that to figure out. A week had passed, and Gabriel hadn't come for us.

A week of waiting for word on the third relic and

wondering what had happened to the celestial who'd saved my life was a week too long.

We needed a plan. We needed to act.

I had to find Shem and call a meeting. If we couldn't get to the third relic, then we needed to make moves to get hold of the fourth.

Wherever that might be.

CHAPTER 3

MICHAEL

"This part of the mall is off limits," Shem says, standing before a reinforced metal door that has been welded shut. "The damage is too severe beyond this point. And that's everything. The whole facility."

It's taken a few days, but by staying in my lane and helping where I can, I've garnered more of Shem's trust. Now I have a map of this place in my head, one I can use when the time is right. "And the tunnels are infested?"

"Yes. Venture forth at your peril. The watchers who've mutated are hungry for flesh. The runes keep them penned in...for now." He leads us away from the restricted zone and back toward the heart of the mall.

"Is Kabiel down there? Is that how you knew where the relic piece was?"

He looks across at me sharply, and for a moment I fear that I've pushed too far, but then he sighs and nods. "Kabiel sacrificed himself to protect this sanctuary. So far, he's staved off devolution and managed to control the watchers in the tunnels. But for how much longer?" He shakes his head. "We need to find the relic pieces."

But there is another way to bring order. One that I will implement. I want to tell him. To share my plans, but he won't understand. He'll see it as a betrayal.

No. I must hold my own counsel for a little longer.

Lights above us flicker and crackle, and we round the corner to find Tumiel and Bastian standing by an open metal box fixed to the wall.

"Is everything all right?" Shem asks.

Bastian grunts in response, his focus on the wires in the metal box.

"Nothing we can't handle," Tumiel says. His gaze flicks to me briefly.

I can tell he doesn't trust me. Yet.

But I don't need his trust if I have Shem's and Rue's.

We pass the pair and head toward the center of the mall. This place with its back corridors and its wide-open spaces filled with shuttered rooms and the scent of human occupation has a certain charm that's absent from the clean, clinical corridors of the tower in the

Golden City. And it's not due to the environment, but due to the people—humans and watchers living side by side in harmony. A far contrast from the way the celestials choose to live alongside humans.

This place is truly something special. There's no doubt that Shem has done good work here.

Work I plan to continue. "I want to help protect this place. I'll be able to do that if you give me my sword." Shem makes a noncommittal sound, and I staunch my irritation. "I won't be able to wield it much longer. My celestial light is dying. I just...It would be nice to hold it one last time..."

"You'll get it once we're ready to go after the final piece of the relic," Shem says.

We've waited a week for Gabriel to bring us the third piece. Waited because Rue has confidence in him, but she doesn't know...She can't know. "I don't think Gabriel is coming. I think something must have gone wrong."

"Yes. I believe you're right. We've waited long enough."

It's taken three days of gently pushing and probing to get him to this point, to admit that we need to move forward on the relic hunt. I need to know where it lies, and I need my sword.

We climb a short flight of stairs and come out on a balcony looking down on an area of the mall that's gloomy. It's in the process of being cleaned to make room for the humans to spread out. A couple of humans look up at Shem and smile.

They smile at him, despite his monstrous visage yet give me nothing but wariness.

Indignation sits hot in my chest. I am a celestial. An Archangel. These people know nothing of who I once was or the power I wielded.

Let them look.

Let them be wary.

It won't be long now until they understand the true magnitude of—

"Once we have three pieces, then we'll have enough power to go after the one hidden in the Golden City," Shem says. "It's what we should have done in the first place."

He's annoyed with Rue, and for some reason, this gives me a stab of satisfaction. I could push him to sit more firmly in his doubts, but my instincts tell me that any word spoken against the female could be detrimental to the tenuous trust I've fostered with him.

Instead, I play the advocate. "Rue was saving your lives by coming with me." There's no denying that the woman has the heart of a lion. I wish that things could be different. That I didn't have to betray her, but the world *must* come first. "She made the right decision at the time based on what she knew."

Once again, Shem makes a non-committal sound, but this time, I sense a hint of approval.

We enter the corridor that will lead us to the central chamber of the mall, where the fountain with its bell is situated. Rue appears, striding toward us, her jaw set in that determined way of hers.

"Shem, we need to talk." Her gaze settles on me for a beat, and even though I sense her tension, there is warmth in her eyes for me.

Guilt writhes in my belly, but I mask it with a smile.

"We need to call a meeting," she says.

"Yes," Shem replies. "I was coming to find you to suggest the same thing."

There's a special heat in the smile that she bestows on him, a private heat that makes me want to look away. "Great minds," she says.

"Yes, Rue, great minds." Her name is a caress on his lips, and something inside me twists painfully.

They are intimate. Of course, I know this. But the way he speaks to her. The way he looks at her...This is more than intimacy, and I know in that moment that I will use it against him when the time is right.

CHAPTER 4

RUE

Shem waited, arms crossed over his powerful chest, while the watchers settled into seats in the cinema room.

His skin, which had been a rose hue when I'd left him to go after the third relic piece, had darkened to a deeper red once more, and the golden highlights in his chestnut hair were gone. He was devolving again, just like the other watchers who were standing on the far side of the platform, farthest from the main exit.

Tumiel's teeth were looking sharper, Sarq's horns were thicker, and Zaq's talons looked longer. How much would they have devolved without my intervention, without being able to feed off the residual energy seeping out from the gaps around that door that I kept closed between myself and the Morningstar's power?

If they hadn't found me in time...

I dreaded to think of them in the tunnels with Kabiel. These males had become my family, and I'd do whatever it took to keep them safe.

"You're thinking too hard," Bastian said from beside me.

I leaned against him and tipped my head so that it touched his shoulder. "I have a lot on my mind."

"You can tell me all about it later on tonight."

I closed my eyes briefly, reveling in the promise of our quality time together. It was more than sex. More than lovemaking. It was a time of shared memories and stories. A time when we remembered our past.

I loved my nights with Bastian, but the seed of dread inside me grew daily knowing that those nights were numbered unless I found a way to save him. I looked up at his strong profile, familiar and beloved to me. I would do it. I would save him.

My stomach dipped with despair.

No. I wouldn't allow it to surface. Not yet.

His hand slipped into mine, and he squeezed gently as if he knew...as if he sensed my thoughts.

Michael caught my eye from across the room. He stood with the watchers, but a little apart from them. His golden hair was brushed back from his face and secured in a bun, and his sapphire eyes were dark with emotions I couldn't define. He dropped me a nod and half a smile before turning his attention to Shem.

Beside me, Bee shifted from foot to foot, impatient for the meeting to start. I'd dragged her in with me, wanting her to be a part of this. She'd already demanded to come on the next relic fragment hunt, so she needed to be a part of the decision-making process, even if it was just to listen.

"Settle down," Shem ordered, and the room fell into silence. "We've waited a week for Gabriel to find us and bring the third piece of the relic to us. He hasn't joined us, and we can only assume that something has gone wrong. We cannot wait any longer."

A murmur of agreement skittered over the crowd, and Shem waited for it to die before continuing. "We'll be moving forward with finding the location." His gaze flitted my way, and my stomach tightened because I knew what we needed to do.

The quickest way to find the location of the relic piece was to help Kabiel with his visions, and that meant going into the tunnels to find him. It meant channeling Morningstar power into him. But the devolved watcher had made it clear how he wanted me to do that...what he wanted from me.

"Once we have the fourth piece," Shem continued, "we'll storm the city using the secret passage. Having that piece should increase the residual power that Rue can produce for us."

"You know this for sure?" Baraqel asked.

"It makes sense," Amaros replied for Shem. "The more pieces we have, the stronger the connection to the Morningstar power. Having another piece, be it the one in the Golden City or the one of unknown location, will provide us with an edge."

"We'll use the secret entrance into the city that bypasses their wards," Shem said.

I looked over at Michael in time to see his jaw tense. My scalp prickled with unease. "Do you have a problem with that, Michael?"

The watchers looked from me to Michael, and I wanted to bite my tongue for speaking out. We needed to foster trust, not doubt.

If Michael was fazed by my question, he didn't show it. He simply exhaled wearily. "Loss of life is always a problem. Many celestials will die simply because they're following the orders of a corrupt power." He took a fortifying breath. "But in the end, it will be worth it."

His concerns made sense, and the others relaxed, accepting his words at face value, just as I wanted to, but my unease remained.

I trusted Michael. He'd protected me and saved my life once we got outside the Golden City. There was no reason to doubt him now.

"That's all I had to say," Shem said, "but Rue has something she needs to add."

I'd told him about the ghost, my most recent sighting, and Mira's concerns, but the others needed to be aware of it too. "We have a creature in our midst. Something that's been stalking me ever since we got back. I thought it was a ghost, but last night, I saw its eyes. Orange eyes, glowing in the dark."

"When?" Bastian asked.

"Just before I fell asleep. I was too tired to stay awake, and this morning, Mira told me someone's been stealing food from a locked room to which only she has the key."

"You saw orange eyes and you simply fell asleep?" Tumiel looked skeptical.

Now that he said it, it did sound odd. "You think I was *made* to fall asleep?"

"Mira thinks that this thing might be stealing food?" Zaq asked.

"It's a possibility. No one else has access to the room, and this thing...I mean, for all we know, it could walk through walls."

"And yet need to eat?" Baraqel gave a snort of disbelief. "I say we stop chasing shadows and focus on the real issue. The relic is all that matters."

This watcher was a pain in my ass. "You're right, we need to go after the fourth relic piece, but we also need to be sure we're not leaving the people here in danger when we do."

"You let us worry about that," Penemue said. "If

there is a presence here, then we will deal with it. Your focus must remain on the relics." He raised his head slightly so that his dark hair parted to reveal brown eyes now ringed in crimson. "We're running out of time."

"If this thing is stalking you, then maybe it will leave with you," Amaros pointed out.

Shem stepped in. "Penemue, you'll focus on finding the food thief. Baraqel, you're in charge of security in our absence."

Baraqel stood taller. "I will do so with honor."

"Everyone, get some rest," Shem said. "I'll have news of when we leave soon enough."

"Zaq, may I have a word?" Penemue asked.

Zaq crossed the room to join him, and they left together, trailing after the others.

Michael, Sarq, Tumiel, and Bee stayed with Shem and me.

"You left Baraqel in charge?" Sarq said. "You trust him completely now?"

"No, but I trust that he'll honor this position of power and do whatever it takes to keep the humans safe in our absence. Baraqel is a watcher who was created to lead, and we need to give him the opportunity to do so. I realize now that I may have stifled him."

"You're going to see Kabiel, aren't you?" Bastian said.

"Yes," Shem replied.

24

"I'm coming with you."

"No. It's better if Rue and I go alone. The devolved watchers are used to my scent, which I can use to mask Rue. Too many bodies and it becomes difficult to remain undetected. Tumiel, Sarq, you know what to do if we don't return."

They both nodded.

I wanted to ask what that was, but my gut told me I probably didn't want to know. But there was something I needed to ask them. "You said the monsters get pulled back to Gehenna when the relic is put back together, and the celestials can return to heaven. What happens if they *don't* leave?"

"Then we make them go," Shem said. "This is not their home."

"And you..." I scanned his face. "Is it your home?"

His jaw ticked. "Watchers belong in a place between heaven and earth."

But not in it.

He would leave.

Leave this earth and leave me.

A pit of nothingness yawned inside me at the prospect of the absence of him, and my instinct was to challenge him, to push. But now wasn't the time or place for this conversation, so I dropped my gaze, not wanting him to see how much that hurt.

"Get some rest, Rue," Shem said. "We'll leave at dawn."

"Why do you have to wait?" Bee asked.

"Because the devolved watchers are nocturnal. Most will be asleep during the day."

Like the monsters. "What if Kabiel is...What if he's gone?"

"Then we'll deal with him, and we'll find another way."

The other way would mean making ourselves vulnerable to detection opening the channel and hoping that it could guide me.

We had to hope that Kabiel was still himself. Our fates depended on it.

CHAPTER 5

GABRIEL

My cell is sparse, designed not only to hold a prisoner but to mentally torture him too. With nothing to stimulate the mind, a captive could spiral into madness quickly, but I have a playground in *my* mind. A space where I can retreat. A garden filled with sunshine and the sweet scent of honeysuckle. A brook bubbles and babbles not far from my perch on a flat rock. From here, I watch the bees fly from flower to flower. Music plays somewhere —an upbeat melody.

I'm content here with my thoughts and beauty all around.

The Dominion cannot reach this part of my mind. They cannot find me here. I doubt they'll have need to come looking for me, though. They have what they need.

Michael betrayed me. Betrayed Rue.

I've exhausted my memory running over every interaction with him over and over, searching for a missed moment of deception. A word, a look, but the only conversation that springs to mind is our interaction on the security floor when Paiter hacked into Dominion security. There'd been a moment when Michael questioned our return to heaven and wondered if we would fit. He'd mentioned how it would be wonderful to be powerful once more. This was the moment I should have had doubts.

Michael the Archangel. Michael with his sword blazing with light. Worshipped by all. I should have known, that given the choice, he would choose power. To be revered. To have status once more. The threat of living on half rations had been too much for him.

But when had he spoken to the Dominion? Had they come to him? No...he would have gone to them. Made a deal at our expense.

I should never have trusted him.

The world is in danger and all I can think about is the human, Rue. The dark-haired vixen with a smart mouth and eyes that pierce my soul. I'd be lying if I said my eagerness to bond with her was purely strategic. I want her in a way I haven't wanted anything in a long time. I'm not sure why, but she's awakened a longing inside me that's been absent for millennia.

I've obviously been trapped in this damn city for too long.

Once my celestial energy dies, they'll come for me. They'll kill me.

I'll die a mortal, and all my planning, all my efforts, will have been for nothing. If Michael gave them my name, he would have given them Erelim's also.

The reaper is probably in the cell beside me along with his team, and it won't be long before they've rooted out the others.

Erelim was supposed to be the back-up plan. The one to take over if I was caught. If they have him, then the movement is over.

How many days have passed?

The vista around me shimmers and melts away, and I'm back in my gray cell, its walls smooth and unmarred without a crack or a stain to provide me with visual stimulation.

But something has changed. Something is different. I sit up, bracing my hands on the narrow cot, eyes on the door.

There's someone out there. My scalp prickles, body tensing, ready for a fight.

The door swings open a moment later, and Erelim fills the frame dressed in his black armor, arcane symbols glowing softly. "I think you've had a little too much down time, don't you?" Erelim says.

The sounds of fighting drift into the room, and my relief is quickly overtaken by urgency. "You can tell me all about how you evaded the Powers once we get out of here."

He nods, his expression solemn. "Take this. You're going to need it. I have more."

It's a vial, one I recognize as the serum we used to give to the sweeper humans. I don't ask any more questions. I know why he's giving this to me. It contains trace amounts of celestial light. Not perfect, but enough to slow down devolution once we escape this place.

I uncap it and drain the liquid before following Erelim out of the door and into a much-needed, bloody fight.

TURNS out there's no need for my skills. Two sentinels lay prone on the ground, knocked out by Erelim's reapers. Five strong, they're a force to be reckoned with.

"Hurry!" A Power stands guard outside the prison block, ushering us to move. "We don't have long before systems come back online. Once that happens, the Dominion will be alerted and there will be no escape."

This Power is helping us?

"You're not the only one who can recruit, Gabriel," Erelim says. "Jayren broke us out as soon as it was safe to do so."

"The main troop has left the city," Jayren says. "They're tracking something important and left me in charge. I managed to pull some files off their systems and shut down tower security for half an hour so we can move unseen, but we must leave now."

But how do we get out? "The passageway will be locked. Michael will have told them about it."

"He did," the Power says. "And it is. Three sentinels are guarding it."

"But we can get through." Erelim's eyes gleam with wicked intention. "Celestials may not have souls like humans, but a scythe is built to separate energy from a physical form."

He is going to tear the celestials out of their bodies. My lips curve in response. "Now this I have to see."

CHAPTER 6

MICHAEL

"You're a celestial, aren't you?" The child peers up at me with wide inquisitive eyes.

I don't want to speak to anyone. I want to go back to my quarters and hide there until it's time to put my plan into motion, so I bypass the child. At least I try, but the creature steps into my path and looks up at me with what can almost be described as defiance before repeating his question.

How old is he? Ten years? Twelve maybe? He waits for my response.

"I am a celestial, yes."

His eyes narrow. "Were you the one who killed all our people on the tracks?"

The purge. This child was there?

His small chest moves up and down with erratic breath, and his eyes gleam with rage as he waits for my confirmation.

I nod. "I was following orders." I'm not sure why I feel the need to explain myself to this tiny human. "It was not an act I enjoyed." Again. What is wrong with me?

"Why are you here?" he demands. "You shouldn't be here after what you did."

"David!" A woman rushes over and gently takes his shoulder. "I told you not to speak to it."

It...She called me an *it*.

She looks up at me with barely concealed hatred. "He's just a child. He doesn't understand the nuances of war. Especially where one side is completely unarmed." She puts her arm around the boy and draws him away, leaving me with a pit in my stomach.

I've leveled cities at heaven's command and felt nothing, and yet now...now this child spawns guilt in my gut over a mere purge.

This will not do.

I have a higher purpose, and nothing can derail that.

I hurry to my quarters and lock the door before retreating to the single wooden chair pushed up against a metal desk. I close my eyes and focus on my purpose, and suddenly I'm back in the chamber of Authority. Blinding, blessed light and celestial energy fill my limbs. I'm on my knees, with the voice of the Dominion in my head.

"You have done well in coming to us with this information, Michael. Shem's plan could ruin us all. But your plan to stop it will put you in the belly of the beast. You do not need to go through with it. We can end the girl now. Without her, Shem will not find the final piece of the relic, and he will never get the piece we hold."

Yes. I went to them. I revealed Gabriel's plan because it was the only way to save us all. I recall my reply to the Dominion's suggestion.

"Shem doesn't need Rue to find the pieces. They have a prophet, and she's channeled enough power into him to allow him to see again. We must cut the head off the snake. Retrieve all the relic pieces and capture Shem. He's the only being who can reforge the Morningstar."

Silence stretches. "You will undertake this task?"

"I will. Once they take me to their base, I will find my sword and use the Word, given to me by the Dominion, to summon my troops with it."

"Then you have our leave to go. You will not be stopped, and once you return, full glory will be yours once more. Once you return, you shall sit at our side where you truly belong.

Where I truly belong.

Yes.

I will claw my way to that seat no matter what it takes, and no human child, no human female, no sanctuary will keep me from my goal.

Sacrifices must be made for the greater good.

That has always been the way.

When the dust settles, this world will understand. When it settles, the humans that remain will thank me.

CHAPTER 7

RUE

Bastian's large hands gripped my hips as I rode him. My body tightened, webs of sensation spreading across my inner thighs. I wanted to throw back my head and abandon myself to the sensation, but that would mean breaking eye contact with him, and I couldn't bring myself to do that. I needed to devour every nuance of his expression—the way his mouth parted on every sound of pleasure and the way his eyes fell to half-mast as he fought his own instinct to close them and sink into himself.

We remained connected, not just in body but in mind too. There was a unique pleasure in that, and when release found us, we experienced it together, completing the circuit in a kiss where we shared our ragged breath and swallowed each other's gasps of gratification.

The afterglow was my favorite part. Just lying in his strong arms, cocooned by his larger frame, safe and warm as our bodies found the same rhythm of breath.

"When you do this with Shem..." Bastian said. "When he's...inside you, do you have to control the channel to stop the Morningstar power coming through?"

"What made you think of that?"

"I'm not sure. It just popped into my head."

We didn't speak about my nights with Shem and what we got up to, just like I didn't speak to Shem about my intimate time with Bastian. They were agreeable to sharing me, but our relationships remained separate.

I was happy to answer his question, though. "I never used to. The first time, it just produced a huge boost in residual power, but that changed."

"Why?"

"I don't know. It feels like the power is becoming stronger, more connected to me and my emotions, but...but I'm also getting better at controlling it."

"Do you think finding the second fragment had anything to do with it? Now that Shem has it in his possession...You two are connected, after all."

"Maybe. I don't really know. All I know is that I have to keep the door to the power closed."

"Door?"

"That's how I see it...Feel it. Like there's this door between it and me. When Shem and I have sex, he connects to the power too. It's always a risk, I suppose, but this...with you...I can let go completely and abandon myself to sensation."

He kissed my throat, my jaw, and finally my lips. "I want to drown in sensation with you, Rue. To milk every moment we have."

A vacuum opened in my heart. "Don't. Don't talk like that."

He sighed and looked deep into my eyes. "We know better than to lie to ourselves. We're survivors, and we know when the road is coming to an end. It isn't giving up, it's accepting fate. I'm at peace with mine, Rue. I need you to be too."

But I couldn't. I couldn't accept that this vibrant man was dying. That the very thing that he'd used to keep so many alive had signed his death warrant.

"There has to be a—"

He cut off my words with his lips, sinking into a kiss that melted my resistance and momentarily calmed the tumult of thoughts churning in my mind. We surfaced only to come together again urgently, because the fire in our blood had been relit and there was only one way to assuage it.

IT HAD to be close to midnight by the time we settled to go to sleep. My body was lethargic and sated, but like always, my mind teemed with activity. "What have you and Tumiel been working on all week?"

"A super-secret project." He slow-blinked as if he was struggling to keep his eyes open.

I should have let him rest, but I wasn't ready to end the night yet. "Too secret to tell me?" I poked his side, and he chuckled.

"Wait, are you..."

His eyes flew wide. "Don't even think about it."

But now that I knew, how could I not?

"Rue..." His voice held warning and authority—the kind of tone he'd used on the younger cadets. But we weren't at the settlement any longer, and he wasn't my superior, and dammit, I needed to hear him laugh—unabashed and unrestrained.

I struck fast, aiming for his sides, and his rich, warm laughter filled the room. "Stop. Hey, stop." He was weak with it, unable to fight me off. He rolled so he was on top of me, and I relaxed, allowing him to press me into the mattress as my hands slipped from his ribcage and slid up to hook around his neck.

"So? This super-secret project?"

He gave me a lazy smile. "Not secret really. We're

clearing out a second exit from the mall. It's always been there, but the doors were jammed. The electrics shot. I've opened it out, and we're working on clearing it of debris and checking it's all stable. I also managed to get to the upper floor where there's some natural light. I think with the right preparation, we might be able to get a greenhouse going, and I've spoken to Tumiel about rounding up some cattle. The monsters can't have gotten them all."

"You want to farm?"

"Yes. Eventually. If we don't make provisions, then the food will run out. We survived all this time due to the export from other settlements. We need to find a way to produce our own. We can do this. We can have this place running like clockwork, self-sufficient in a few months."

He was amazing, and he was mine. Mine.

"I love you, Bastian." He froze. A chest-still, unbreathing kind of stillness that made my throat ache. But I'd said it, and I'd say it again. "I think that I've loved you for some time now."

He closed his eyes and exhaled through his nose. "I don't remember a time when I didn't love you."

His words, which should have brought me only joy, settled on me like an ominous weight.

"I'm sorry," he said. "I'm sorry I have to leave you."

Dammit. I didn't want to cry. Not now. Not after such a beautiful evening. I didn't want to taint our time together with sadness, but the tears came anyway. I forced my lips into a smile. "You'll never leave me, Bastian. You're a part of me now. Forever."

He kissed away my tears and rolled off me before pulling me into his arms, his chest to my back. I closed my eyes and drank in this moment. The sensation of his skin against mine, the way our hearts beat in time to each other, chests rising and falling in tandem. I told myself that I'd have this memory. Always. That it was okay to accept fate, but the stubborn bitch inside me wouldn't let go.

I couldn't lose him.

Not yet.

His body was broken, but his soul...His soul was intact and...Wait...Jamie had been dying too and now... Now he was whole. Reborn because he'd died with the serum in his blood, and a celestial couldn't be killed by the purge.

I could save Bastian! All we needed was serum in his body and a celestial to purge him.

I looked over my shoulder, eager to share this news with him, but his eyes were closed and his breathing steady and deep. Sleep had already taken him, but I was too excited to wait.

I had to speak to Michael about this.

Now.

CHAPTER 8

BEE

Tumiel adds the finishing touches to the last symbol on the storeroom wall, then hides it with a sack of flour.

"You really think these symbols will help trap the ghost?"

"Runes," Tumiel says with a closed-lip smile.

He's taken to doing that the last couple of days, probably because his teeth are becoming sharper. Devolution, they call it.

I want to tell him that I don't care. That what he looks like doesn't matter to me, but his feelings about his appearance aren't to do with me. They're his insecurities, and I have no right poking at them. All I can do is show him that it doesn't bother me by not changing how I am with him.

Penemue stands on the threshold, scanning the room through a curtain of dark hair. Now if anyone has the creepy factor, it's this guy. He moves like a shadow in permanent stealth mode.

"Yes," he says. "This should work. If the creature is a spirit or otherworld entity of some kind, the runes will hold it here and we can question it."

I follow Tumiel out of the storeroom and wait while he locks it. There's another symbol on the outside of the door. This one isn't hidden.

"Wait, won't it see that?" I point at the rune.

"It's hidden to otherworld eyes," Tumiel says. "If the creature gets inside and is trapped, this symbol will glow and tell us as much."

We head back to the dining hall, where Mira and Amaros wait.

"Now what?" Mira asks.

"Now we wait," Penemue says. "Go about the rest of your evening. We'll check on the storeroom after midnight."

Tumiel hands Mira the key. "Meet us here just after midnight."

I check the large clock hung across from us. It's just past nine pm. Almost three hours to kill. It's Rue's evening with Bastian so she'll be busy, and the thought of hanging out in my room alone doesn't appeal to me. Sissy is an early to bed kinda gal so...I look up at Tumiel, who's watching me with a strange, almost speculative expression, and smile. "You wanna hang out for a while?"

His emerald eyes warm beneath dark lashes. "I would like that. What would you like to do?"

Just being close to him is enough but saying that is kinda creepy. "We could go bowling." There's an arcade and bowling alley in the sector of the mall that's being opened up.

"I've never...bowled."

"I can teach you. We had a basic setup back in the settlement. Nothing fancy or automated like the one here, but..." I shrug. "It'll be fun."

Tumiel smiles with his eyes. "Bowling it is, then."

My heart flutters, and I drop my gaze. Why do I suddenly feel shy?

THE ARCADE IS dark and quiet, the machines dead without power. This part of the mall holds all the leisure activities. There are salons and a spa and some fast-food places. Tumiel explains that they'd struggled getting the electricity running to this area, but Bastian is working on that problem, and most of the stores now have power. They'll be turning it on only if needed, though, and in the next week or so, the people will be given the chance to move to this sector and spread out a little, to be allocated proper spaces to themselves and not have to share. Sissy can have a school, and we can maybe get one of the salons operational for haircuts and beauty treatments. We can build a community here. A safe place to expand from once we claim our world back.

"What are you thinking?" Tumiel asks as we approach the lanes. "You're very quiet."

"Are you saying I'm usually too chatty?"

"Not at all. I happen to enjoy the sound of your voice."

Enjoy. Not *like* but enjoy. He has such a way with words. A way of making me feel appreciated and valued. He made me feel good about myself, not that I needed the validation, but still, it was nice.

"So what were you thinking?" he asks again.

"I'm thinking how wonderful this place will be once we're done fixing it up. How it could be the start of a new era."

"Yes," Tumiel says. "This place is home now."

"It gives me hope."

"This place *is* hope. It's the last stand, and we must protect it at all costs. But the Golden City will soon belong to humanity. We will make sure of it."

I suppress a shudder. "I'd be happy never to go back there again."

I've shared my experience with him. The gaps in my memory and the strange dreams that have surfaced since. They had me in one of their mixers. They played with my mind and my emotions.

They used me.

I escaped, but so many didn't. "There are others trapped there. We've got to free them."

"And we will." Tumiel picks up a bowling ball and holds it easily in his large hand. "And what do we do with these?"

I pick up a second ball and smile up at him. "Let me show you."

The next hour passes too quickly, filled with laughter and a lightness that I haven't felt in years. Being with Tumiel is easy and comfortable but exciting at the same time. The flutter in my belly comes and goes, but I'm becoming used to it now.

After bowling, we sit and talk, and the time slips by until Tumiel stands with a sigh and holds out his hand to me.

"We should go meet the others."

"It's midnight already?" I slip my hand into his, ignoring the frisson of awareness that shoots through me.

"Yes, Bee. But as you humans say, time flies when one is having fun."

He reaches out and tucks a tendril of hair behind my ear. "I enjoy your company, and I'd like to have more of it. I wish that we had more time to simply… be."

My heart sinks, but I refuse to let our uncertain future dampen the mood. "There'll be time once we fix what's broken." The shadows in his eyes warn me that might not be the case. Rue asked Shem what would happen to the watchers once the Morningstar was fixed and the world was put to rights, and he blatantly said that the watchers didn't belong here. But so much has changed.

Where they belong can be changed too when the time comes.

"IT'S GLOWING." Mira points at the symbol on the storeroom door. "There's something in there."

"Unlock it," Penemue says.

"Won't that let it out?" Mira asks.

"No, it's surrounded by runes and they act as a net. It can't get out unless we remove one of the symbols."

Mira unlocks the door and stands back quickly.

I don't blame her for being wary. There's an unknown entity beyond that door, and I wouldn't want to be the first one inside with it either.

Penemue and Tumiel step forward. They're going in. My pulse beats harder. "Be careful."

Tumiel nods, a signal for Penemue to open the door. They duck inside and close it behind them.

"They'll be fine," Amaros says, but his tone is tight with concern.

"You don't sound so sure."

"That thing, whatever it is, has been here for days. If it wanted to hurt someone, it would have done so. We just need to find out what it wants."

Once again, he sounds like he's convincing himself. I don't like this.

The door opens, and Tumiel steps out. "It's not inside."

"What?" Mira looks past him into the room. "But the symbol was glowing."

Penemue emerges, shaking his head. "It was definitely inside the room, but the runes didn't hold it."

Mira looks from Tumiel to Penemue. "What does that mean?"

I can guess. "It means that this thing is stronger than we thought."

CHAPTER 9

RUE

The security corridor was silent and empty as I made my way quickly toward Michael's room. We'd housed him with us to keep him out of view of the general population. The people here needed time to get used to him and accept that he was on our side. The survivors of the purge needed time to come to terms with the fact that Michael had been following orders—trapped in a cycle of awfulness just like all of us.

They'd come around once he'd proven himself to them. Once he'd saved their lives and shown them that not all celestials were monsters.

I'd seen the way they looked at him though. Disgust. Fear. Anger. It wasn't an easy task for him being here, but he believed in the cause. He was part of the team, and I'd do whatever it took to help him adjust.

But right now, I needed something from him.

It was only when I got to his door that it hit me that it was almost one in the morning. Did celestials sleep? Did it matter if they did or didn't? I should wait till sunup, but fuck it.

I knocked, and Michael answered almost immediately, as if he'd been standing on the other side of the door waiting for me to decide what to do.

It was still strange seeing him in a T-shirt and joggers. With his wings hidden, he might pass for human. A beautiful human with hair that looked like it was made from spun gold and...Nope. Even dressed like this, his otherness was obvious.

"Rue, is everything all right?" He peered down the dark corridor then fixed his inquisitive sapphire gaze on me.

"Can we talk?"

"Of course." He stepped back to let me into the room.

It was a small, clean space, made to look smaller by the large male standing in it. The bed was neatly made, the covers unwrinkled, which meant he'd been awake. Probably sitting in the chair by the small desk in the corner of the room. There was a book on the table. Placed face down. I couldn't read the title.

He followed my gaze. "There's a bookstore here. One of the humans, Mira, I think, said it was all right to take a book if I brought it back."

"What's it about?"

"I'm not sure yet. One moment it reads like a story about revenge and in other moments of love and redemption." He looked genuinely confused.

"It can be all those things, you know. Humans are complicated."

He smiled wryly. "Yes, I'm beginning to understand that. But I doubt you came here to discuss my reading choices. What did you need me for?"

"I want you to help Bastian."

He canted his head. "Help him? How?"

"He was on the serum like Jamie, and now...Now he's dying. I'm not sure how long he has left, but I know you can help him." I didn't want to see sympathy on his face. Sympathy didn't solve anything. "You can save him by doing what you did to Jamie."

He blinked sharply. "You want me to *purge* him?"

I pushed back my shoulders. "Yes. If we can get some serum into his body and you purge him, then he can be reborn and—"

"Slow down." He took a step toward me, his beautiful face etched with concern.

I took a breath, staring up at him hopefully.

"Rue, even if I somehow managed to get ahold of

serum, purging takes more than one celestial. It takes a troop at full celestial capacity."

"But once Gabriel finds us, once he brings the celestials that are helping him, you'd be able to do it. Gabriel's been planning a rebellion for decades. He'll have a way of getting hold of celestial light."

Michael dropped his gaze to the floor. He was considering it, and hope fluttered in my chest.

When he looked up, his expression was probing. "A purge will wipe all Bastian's memories. He won't remember you. He won't remember any of the things that make him who he is. Are you prepared for that?"

I was aware of this. Aware and willing to deal with it. "But he'll get to live, and that's all that matters."

Michael's gaze flicked over my head. "Bastian..."

I turned to find Bastian in the doorway, an undecipherable expression on his face.

"Bastian, I was just—"

"I heard," he bit out. "I heard it all. My question is, do I get a say?"

Why did he sound angry? "What? Of course. I was going to tell you, but you were asleep, and I was excited so—"

"You thought you'd get the ball rolling without checking with me first."

What was his problem? "*Checking* with you?"

"To see what *I* want. If I even want to do this."

He wasn't making sense. "I don't understand, why

wouldn't you? You'd get to live. You'll have a chance to—"

"To what?" His jaw ticked. "Be a blank slate with no memories?"

"We can make new memories. Fall in love again and—"

"And what if we *don't* fall in love again? Love doesn't just spout out of nowhere. It comes with shared experiences. It comes with being able to connect through thick and thin. Until then, it's simply infatuation. I love you because of who I know you to be. For all the things I've seen you do. For all the moments we've shared. If I do this. If I lose my memories, then all of that...All of the things I felt will be *gone*. I won't be me. Not anymore."

He wasn't looking at the bigger picture. At the fact that we'd have a second chance. At the fact that if we did this, then he'd still be here. Existing. Breathing. "But you'll *live*. There'll be time for us to grow together and make new experiences. To fall in love all over again." I crossed to him, pleading with my eyes. "Bastian, please..."

He met my gaze with cold, angry eyes. "I told you that I was at peace with my fate. I thought you understood that."

"Yes, of course I did, but now that we have a solution, a way to save you, we don't have to accept fate. Bastian, you don't have to die. We can be together."

"No, Rue. We can't because the thing that comes back, the person that's reborn, it won't be me."

His words struck a chord inside me, but it wasn't a chord I wanted to listen to. He was being stubborn and argumentative. "What is wrong with you? Don't you want to live?"

He searched my face as if he couldn't believe what he was hearing. "Yes, Rue, of course I do, but not if the cost is the memory of us."

I didn't want to understand. I didn't want to accept this. We had a solution. We had hope, and I wanted to hold on to that, and he was ruining it. "Damn you!"

I shoved past him and ran down the corridor. I couldn't be around him now because my heart was breaking all over again, shattering the fragile hope that I'd been building inside it.

I slipped into Shem's room and crawled into his bed. It was warm with the imprint of him, and I breathed him in, allowing his scent to calm the raging tumult of emotion inside me.

The door opened a few minutes later.

"You can sleep here if you like," Shem said, a hint of amusement in his tone.

"I wasn't asking permission."

"If it makes you feel better to take out your frustration on me, then so be it."

Fuck my life. I couldn't even be angry and snippy without feeling guilty. "I'm sorry."

"I spoke to Bastian." The bed dipped as he got in behind me. "He's made his wishes clear."

My throat pinched. "Yeah, he wants to die."

"He doesn't *want* to die, Rue. But he's accepted that he will. You're making it harder for him by fighting it. There is no way to save him, not without losing everything that makes him the man you love."

My thoughts were a tumultuous mess governed by emotion. "Are you saying that Jamie...that he'll never be the same?"

"Humans are shaped by their life experiences, Rue. You know this."

I squeezed my eyes shut as if that could block out the truth of his words and take away the guilt that was now burrowing its way into my chest. "I fucked up, didn't I?"

He put his arm around my waist and pulled me against him. "You're human. And there is nothing wrong with that. Bastian understands. You can speak to him tomorrow before we go into the tunnels. There are many things we have no control over, so let's focus our energies on the things that we do."

He was right. The one thing we could control was our effort to fix the Morningstar, and maybe along the way, we'd find a solution to save Bastian that *didn't* involve stripping him of his memories, because I wasn't ready to accept fate.

"Are you really going to leave after it's all done?"

My voice sounded small and vulnerable, and I hated that, but I needed to know for sure. I needed to be mentally and emotionally prepared.

His sigh was a soft exhalation skating over my skin. "I'm not sure that I'll have a choice."

"And if you have a choice?"

He kissed my shoulder. "If I have a choice, then I'll stay. I'll stay with you, Rue."

My eyes heated. "I'd like that. I'd like that a lot."

The shadows across the room shifted, and my heart shot into my throat. I gripped Shem's arm, digging my nails into his skin. "The ghost is here."

CHAPTER 10

T he ghost moved again—a dark smudged shape hidden in the shadows. "It's here, Shem."

Shem tensed behind me. "Where?"

"Across the room, between the desk and the dresser."

He was silent for several beats. "I don't see anything."

But it was there. I could see the humanoid shape clearly now. It moved again, and I opened my mouth to tell Shem, but he was already across the room, grabbing at the darkness with a low menacing growl vibrating in his chest.

The energy in the room spiked. I caught a flash of orange, felt a pressure on my chest, and then the thing was gone.

Shem rushed to the door and yanked it open. "Where the fuck did it go?"

I sat up, pulse pounding in my head. "You saw it?"

"Yes. I saw something."

The way he said it implied he hadn't expected to see anything, which meant... "You didn't believe me?"

"I believed that you *thought* you saw something, but now...Now I've seen it, I know it's real."

He'd taken my word for it even when he had doubts, and that...that was priceless.

He closed the door and strode over to the bed. "I think I touched it," he said. "I touched it and felt fear and...anger." He climbed into bed and pulled me into his arms. "Sleep and I'll watch over you. If it comes back, I'll deal with it."

The thing was incorporeal, but in that moment, I had no doubt that if it tried to hurt me, Shem would find a way to hurt it back.

I KNOCKED on Bastian's door at six am, knowing he'd be awake. The guy was an early riser, always had been. He opened the door, fully dressed and showered.

"Hey." He held out his arms, and I stepped into them. "I'm sorry about last night."

"So am I."

"No. You were trying to help. I get that."

I rubbed my cheek against the soft worn fabric of his shirt "I was being pushy."

He sighed and stroked my hair. "Yes. You were, but I understand why. I love you, Rue."

"I love you too."

And that was all we'd say about it because Bastian wasn't one to hold a grudge or dwell. This was him drawing a line beneath the argument.

"Rue, we should go," Shem said from down the hall.

"You'll be careful," Bastian addressed Shem.

"Always," Shem replied.

The males shared a look before Bastian released me. "I'll see you this afternoon."

Shem led the way off the security floor and toward the main section of the mall. We took the broken escalators to the floor below then crossed to the exit that led to the red door and the tunnels beyond.

I didn't mind the route to and from the mall, but the deeper tunnels weren't somewhere I wanted to venture. They were home to the devolved watchers. Home to Kabiel, a watcher clinging desperately to his sense of self, and they would be home to Shem and all the other watchers if we didn't fix things soon.

Shem stopped at the red door and turned to me.

"The watchers in the tunnels will be sleeping now, so we want to be as quiet as possible. We'll be taking a slightly different route to Kabiel, and I'd like you to climb onto my back for the journey."

I didn't question why. This was his forte. "Fine."

"If we're spotted and anything comes after us, do not scream. Tuck your head against my shoulder and hold on tight. Let me deal with it."

"Understood."

He gently gripped my chin and tilted my face up. "Understood? I remember a time, not too long ago, when you'd fight me tooth and nail over everything."

I smiled sweetly up at him. "But that was before I realized you weren't a dick and accepted that I *wanted* your dick."

He snorted, eyes dancing with mirth. "You and your filthy mouth."

"You have no idea what I can do with this filthy mouth."

He sucked in a breath, chest rumbling in that almost purr that he made when aroused. "Dammit, woman, this is not the time or place." He leaned in, his blue eyes dark with desire. "Pheromones have a scent, you know."

Shit. "I'm sorry."

"Hold that thought, though. You can demonstrate your filthy mouth's skills once we get back."

Damn, he made me hot. I stepped back and took a breath to clear my head. "Okay, let's get this done."

SHEM MOVED FAST through the tunnels with me on his back. Up pipes and along them too. There was no way I'd have been able to navigate this route on foot. He made it look easy, but the tension and movement of the muscle beneath my body told me just how hard it was.

We finally dropped down a shoot and into a room I recognized as Kabiel's lair. Although *lair* made it sound ominous. As if he was some kind of villain, which he wasn't.

A single oil lamp held the darkness at bay, illuminating the downy nest that Kabiel slept in. But the nest was empty.

The hairs on my nape quivered, warning me that the nest might be empty, but the room wasn't.

"Kabiel," Shem said. "We need to talk."

"It took you long enough to come and see me," Kabiel said from somewhere in the darkness. "You've been back for days."

"And how do you know that?" Shem asked.

"I have my eyes and ears."

Had his voice moved? Wait, was it coming from somewhere above us? There were pipes running along the ceiling of this room, but the lamp was burning so low it was impossible to see them right now.

A shiver ran over my skin, and I moved closer to Shem.

"You're frightening Rue," Shem said. "Show yourself."

"You don't want to see me, especially if you're worried that I might frighten your little human."

His voice sounded different when he said the word *human*. The tone was wet and hungry.

I pressed closer to Shem, wanting nothing more than to get out of here, and if it hadn't been necessary to be here, I'd have suggested just that. Instead, I gritted my teeth and fixed my attention on the spot where his voice was coming from.

"I'm not afraid, Kabiel. Please show yourself so we can talk."

His chuckle was a bubbling, mirthless sound. "Well, if you insist." His face emerged from the shadows, an upside-down oval that ended in a sharp point. His eyes were cold and flat, his mouth thinner and wider. There was something insidious about him now that sent a chill shooting through my bones.

I caught the impression of his spider legs, still clinging to the ceiling in the shadows. Silver threads glinted in the lamplight as he shifted.

Oh fuck...was that...Was that a web?

"You've been busy," Shem said flatly.

"It's a way to pass the time," Kabiel replied.

"We need your help," Shem said.

"Of course you do. A prophecy. But there is a cost, you know that."

This was my cue. "I know. I'm willing to pay it."

"Are you? Don't you want to hear the cost?"

"I know what it is. A kiss." Fuck my life. "Let's do this."

"A kiss?" he sneered. "A kiss will hardly suffice. Look at me! Look what I'm becoming. I'll need more. I'll need to bathe in the power, if only for a moment."

The chill in my bones congealed to ice. "What... what are you saying?"

He shifted closer, and I bit back a yelp.

His eyes blazed with the fire of rage for a moment before going dull and cold once more. "I need what you give to him." He jabbed a finger toward Shem.

Shem's growl was a sound of pure malevolent rage as he placed himself between us. "You don't *need* that. You *want* it. You want it so that you can feel less like the monster you're becoming, but the fact that you can ask it means you're already a fucking monster."

Kabiel recoiled, his spider legs tapping across the stone. He curled in on himself quivering in a way that made me grit my teeth and curl my hands into fists.

"You don't need it," Shem said, his tone softer now.

"You're better than that, Kabiel. All you need is a touch and a moment bathing in the open doorway. She can give you that. She's stronger now. Able to control the channel better."

Kabiel retreated into the darkness. "The others will come."

"No, they won't," Shem said. "Rue has mastered control of the door. She can close it just as quickly as it opens. They won't have time to sense it."

I loved that he had such confidence in me, but I wasn't feeling so sure. It would take a huge burst of power to restore Kabiel to a state where he might be able to receive a prophecy.

"Rue?" Shem watched me with a frown, waiting for me to confirm his words, no doubt.

I had to make this work. "I can help you, Kabiel. Can you...Can you come down here please?"

Tap, tap, tap.

I held myself still, focusing not on the sound of his spider legs or on the fact that he was approaching but on the warm place inside me that wanted nothing more than to save lives.

Kabiel appeared in the lamplight, the top half of his body, the humanoid half, illuminated by soft amber hues. But his skin looked leathery and patchy—crimson in places, blackened and browned in others where the devolution was taking hold. His head bowed as if in shame, and my heart ached for him.

"Kabiel, look at me."

He slowly raised his head and peered at me with mournful eyes. "I don't want to lose myself. I don't want to hurt anyone, but I'm so hungry. Always hungry."

The torment in his tone clawed at me. He was fighting so hard to remain tethered to the watcher he once was. I had to buy him more time. I had to help.

I approached, and his body shivered as if in anticipation. Revulsion gripped my nape, trying to hold me back, but I fought it and pressed forward.

"You won't devolve, Kabiel. I won't let you. We'll find the pieces and put them back together. We will fix this. I swear it."

Shem made a soft sound of protest, as if he was unhappy with me making such a promise, but I had to. I had to swear it and believe it or else all was lost.

I moved closer and tipped my chin up to look Kabiel in the eye, taking a moment to scan his terrifying face—the mandibles that poked out of his jaw and curved toward his mouth, the sharp bridge of his nose, and the cold reptilian edge to his eyes.

He was drowning, but I was going to save him.

I reached up tentatively to touch his cheek, keeping my gaze locked with his and ignoring the rough texture of his skin. "Are you ready?"

His front legs tapped on the stone around us, and I suppressed a shudder.

"I'm ready."

I closed my eyes and sank deep into that place inside me that connected to the Morningstar power. The door waited, firmly closed yet shimmering with the residue of power that I was unable to block completely. This residue fuelled Shem and through him the troop of watchers under his command.

I wished I could do more. Feed all the watchers power, but to do so could drain me. Possibly even kill me.

This...this would have to be enough. I opened the door a crack, controlled and slow, body trembling as the power pushed through in a steady, eager stream. Easy. Control it. Let it out.

My fingers heated, and Kabiel cried out, the sound one of pain and pleasure combined. My vision blazed white as the sharp stream of power channeled through me and into Kabiel.

"Rue!" Shem's warning had me slamming the door closed.

My hand slipped from Kabiel's cheek, and my knees buckled.

"I've got you." Shem scooped me up. "Kabiel?"

I blinked away the black dots in my vision and studied my handiwork. His mandibles were gone, as was the leathery look to his skin, which was now a rosy hue. His pale eyes were no longer cold and hungry. No longer the eyes of a predator. They filled with intelligence and gratitude.

"I feel...better," he said.

"Good," Shem said. "Now have a vision."

Kabiel snorted softly. "It doesn't work that way, Shem, and you know it. The visions come to me. I do not go to them."

"Then you'd better hope they come quickly," Shem said. "Because we're running out of time. We need the fourth relic piece before we storm the city to claim the final piece."

"And what if your secret entrance has been compromised? Gabriel has not come. Maybe the Dominion have him. Maybe they know of the passage."

"You *have* been listening in," Shem said dryly. "Yes, all possibilities. But we're running out of options."

"Agreed." Kabiel's gaze dropped to me and softened. "I will find you as soon as I'm guided."

But there was something that had been niggling at me for a while now, and it came to the fore, suddenly prompting me to ask, "Didn't you see it?"

He frowned. "See what?"

"The fall of heaven? The fracture of the Morningstar?"

Shem's grip on me tightened. "Kabiel, you don't have to dwell on it."

"No." Kabiel clenched his jaw. "I wish to answer. I did not see it. In fact, I saw no visions for months leading up to that moment."

No visions when he was filled with celestial light,

connected to his power with such a dramatic event looming. That made no sense unless...

"The djinn? Maybe she did something to block it?"

"Djinn?" Kabiel looked confused. "What djinn?"

Shem let out a ragged sigh, and it hit me that maybe he'd already made this connection but was trying to avoid talking about it.

I peered up at him, noting the tightness around his mouth. "I'm sorry."

"Don't be," he said gruffly. "You have no reason." Then to Kabiel, "Priyana was no human." He filled Kabiel in on Jilyana, which was Priyana's real name. She was the djinn the Dominion had hired to betray Shem and trick him into fragmenting the Morningstar. "It was my fault. I fell prey to her lies. I brought this on us."

"No, brother. The Dominion are the villains here, and they will pay with their lives. Go now. I will come to you once I have news. Once the power grants me a vision to guide us."

Shem nodded. "Very well, but I should take the cargo with me now."

"Are you worried I'll devolve and make it impossible for you to get to it?" Kabiel said dryly.

What were they talking about?

"Yes," Shem said bluntly. "I would be a fool not to consider it."

"A valid concern. The devolution seems to have sped up." He retreated into the shadows and emerged a moment later carrying a familiar oblong object bundled in thick fabric.

Michael's sword.

CHAPTER 11

MICHAEL

I can feel the presence of my sword even before I open the door to let Shem in. He has it wrapped in thick brown fabric because it's the only way he can carry it.

It calls to me, but I temper my eagerness to take it from him.

"Shem?" I glance at the wrapped object and frown, as if I'm unsure what it is.

"I think you should have this back." Shem holds it out to me like an offering.

My breath stalls as I reach for it, afraid that this is a trick. That he'll snatch it away at any moment.

He doesn't, and in the next moment, my sword is in my hand.

Mine once more. "Thank you."

"Thank you for saving Rue's life. For bringing her back to us. You made the right choice, Michael, and we're glad to have you on our side."

I ignore the prickle of guilt that skates over my skin. Shem is too astute, and if I allow myself to acknowledge it, he'll see it. And if he asks about it, I won't be able to lie without him knowing.

I hold the sword, still wrapped in the fabric, loosely at my side, acting as if it isn't the most important thing that's happened to me in weeks. Acting as if this isn't a pinnacle moment. "Did you speak to Kabiel?"

I'm surprised how normal I sound even though my pulse is thudding hard in my throat.

"Yes. He'll find us when he has a vision."

"How long will that be?"

Shem sighs and shrugs. "I don't know. The visions find him. It could be hours. It could be days. Weeks even."

Hours I can manage. Maybe a day or two, but any longer than that and I'm afraid I won't have enough celestial light in me to use the word and summon the Dominion's troops.

Damn Shem and his guardedness. He kept my sword from me, and he still hasn't revealed the location of the two relic pieces in his possession. Asking again, now that I have the sword, might raise suspicions, and in honesty, the relics won't matter when the only person that can make them whole again is dead.

RUE

I found Bee face down on her bed, fully clothed and snoring loudly. At least she'd kicked off her boots before passing out.

I set a cup of coffee on her bedside table, and she rolled over with a snort and wiped drool from her cheek.

"Wheresit?" She snorted again before her eyes popped open. "Fuck, what time issit?"

I bit back a smile. "Late one?"

She made a face, wiping at the wrinkles on her cheek left by the crumpled bedsheet. "Trying to catch the ghost."

"It was in Shem's room sometime after midnight."

"Fucker." She sat up and rubbed her face to wake herself up. "It was in the storeroom again too. But it got away. We had runes up and everything."

"The runes didn't hold it?"

"Nope." She reached for the coffee. "I need this. Wait...have you been to the tunnels yet?"

"Just got back."

She took a small sip of the steaming coffee. "And?"

"And now we wait for Kabiel to have a vision."

"Did you have to..." She made a kissy face.

"No. Not this time."

She looked relieved on my behalf. "How long will it take for him to get a vision?"

"I have no idea. He doesn't control them, but now that he's a little more himself, they might find him."

"And then we go after the relic."

"Yes."

"Good because I'm getting itchy feet. I need to roam, even if it is out there." She sipped her coffee again. "Where's Shem?"

"He went to find Michael and give him back his sword."

"About time." She shifted her ass to sit with her back against the headboard. "We need to show him that we trust him so he can feel a part of this group."

"Being a part of this group will take time. You weren't there when he purged our people. It was awful. Javier's gone because of it, along with many others. The survivors of that purge only know Michael as a killer. They haven't seen any other side of him. They don't understand the power the Dominion has over its celestials. I hated him too before the Golden City. I'd have happily stabbed him in the face."

She frowned, clearly annoyed. "Then we'll need to explain it to them. We need Michael in this war."

I wasn't about to argue with her. "What's your plan for the day?"

"Working on the new section of the mall with Tumiel and Bastian. You?"

"I promised Sissy I'd give the kids a safety talk about the outside."

"Meet for lunch?"

"Definitely."

IT WAS A STRANGE HOUR, speaking to the children. Back at the settlement when I'd gone in to talk to Sissy's class about being a scout, there'd been excitement and questions. They'd been interested in my stories of near-death adventure, but this time, the mood was solemn.

These children had seen death. Their shelter had been shattered.

The survival talk was just that—a list of things to do if the mall was overrun with monsters.

Every child was instructed to pack a bag and keep it at a spot where they could grab it easily. The rendezvous point for an emergency was by the fountain for now, but I was sure that would change once Bastian and Tumiel finished working on their secondary escape route.

I left the class with a weight on my chest because there would be no innocence of youth for these children. They'd been forced to grow up too fast. To know a kind of fear that no child should be forced to face.

Many were orphans, taken in by the adults who remained.

Our world, our species was dying, and we had to save it.

I found Bee at what had become our table. She'd already grabbed me a sandwich and a coffee.

"You look like someone told you your puppy died," she said around a mouthful of food.

"I'm fine. I just...I need to do something, Bee. I need to get out there and fix our world."

"I know what you mean." The soft crackling of static rose from beneath the table. "Oops." Bee fumbled in the pocket of her overalls, and the sound stopped. "Radio. We were in the new tunnels, and Bastian gave me a radio to keep in touch."

"How is the tunnel going?"

"Still some clearing to do. They're putting in these emergency lights now. It won't be the first option for escape, though. It comes out *inside* the city so not the safest exit, but if our main route is compromised, we can use this one."

There was a lightness about her, a brightness in her eyes that lifted the weight on my chest. "You sound like you had fun today."

"It felt good to be doing something useful again."

"I know what you mean."

"Now eat up." She picked up her sandwich and took another hearty bite as if to demonstrate.

We ate in silence for several minutes as the dining hall got busier. By the time we were done, the place was teeming.

I took our empty plates and cups over to the kitchens, where one of the workers, Henry, took them off me. "No dessert today, I'm afraid," he said. "We're running low on flour, but watcher scouts left a few hours ago. Hopefully they'll bring something useful back."

If Bastian could get a greenhouse up and running, and if the watchers could find a plot of land that we could farm, then food wouldn't be such a problem.

We drifted away from the kitchens.

"Want to come work in the tunnels?" Bee asked.

I had no other plans for the day. "Sure."

We headed into the main chamber where the dried-up fountain sat. Several children ran around it playing tag, and a couple of adults who'd claimed a set of table and chairs nearby chatted amiably while watching over the little ones.

The main chamber led off to various wings of the mall. This was the hub—the heart of this place—and right now, it was filled with children's laughter. The sound lifted my mood and brought a smile to my face.

"I missed this," Bee said.

"Yeah, me too."

"Rue. Bee." Michael strode across the room toward us. "I have my sword back, thanks to you two."

"I heard," Bee said. "About time. You're part of the team now."

Michael smiled. "Yes. And as part of the team, I'd like to help more. When we came in through the tunnels, I noticed some points of concern."

I frowned up at him. "What do you mean?"

"Areas where the structure seemed unstable. I was hoping you might take me back through so that I could have a closer look. It's not too far past the red door."

Leaving the mall and heading past the red door was only for emergencies or with watcher approval. "Have you spoken to Shem about it?"

"Of course," he said smoothly. "But he's busy right now. He suggested I find you."

My scalp prickled. "He did?"

"Yes, is that a problem?" He frowned, looking confused.

"No. Not at all." There was no leaving without watcher approval, but if Shem had said it was okay... "Let's go."

CHAPTER 12

RUE

I didn't like being past the red door. Not like this. Not without Shem. My gut was in knots. The metal grill ceiling was coming up, and after that, we'd be at the steps leading to the long tunnel that ran past the arch that was covered in runes to keep the devolved at bay.

I'd had my fair share of these tunnels for the day. "How much farther?"

Michael stopped and scanned the ceiling, looking for whatever cracks he might have noticed on the way in. Then he stepped back with a sigh. "Here will do."

The stone walls looked fine to me. "I don't see any cracks."

"I'm sorry," he said.

Ice gripped my nape. "What?"

"I didn't want to lie to you. I have no choice. You'll be safe here. I'll come back for you when it's over." He began to back up toward the red door, which was several meters away.

"Michael, what are you doing?" Bee demanded.

She took a step forward, and Michael held up his hand. "Stop. I don't want to hurt you, but I will do so to protect you."

Energy emanated off him, and the lethal glint in his eyes warned that he wasn't messing around.

My heart sank. "What have you done?"

"What needs to be done. The sentinels have been summoned and will be with us shortly. You'll be safe here. They'll come through the mall, cutting a path through the earth."

No... "You...you used the sword somehow..."

Bee shook her head. "You wouldn't. You're a good guy." Her voice trembled.

Michael turned his attention to her, his sapphire gaze softening, almost pleading. "Yes, Bee. I am. Even though I might seem like a monster to you right now. You'll understand soon enough. I won't let any harm come to you. Either of you."

He was betraying us. He was working for the Dominion.

Nausea rolled in my belly. "You came with us so you could find our hideout. You wanted the relics."

His gaze flicked to me. "The relics would have been a bonus, but I don't need them. All I need is to eliminate Shem and his watchers. To squash his tiny rebellion."

He talked about killing Shem and the watchers so calmly as if he was telling us he liked taking long walks.

A bubble of fear and anger expanded in my chest. "You bastard. You fucking bastard."

His jaw hardened, eyes darkening with anger. "Call me whatever you want. It makes no difference. If I could spare Shem and his watchers their fate so that they could revel in the glory to come, then I would. It's unfortunate that they will not survive to see it, but you can. You can both be a part of my new world."

"Michael, I don't understand," Bee said quickly. "I thought you wanted to help us free the humans. To stop the Dominion and return to heaven." Her tone was soft and tremulous, a contrast to my harsh, abrasive one.

Michael tore his gaze from me and fixed his attention on Bee. I caught movement at her hip, her fingers flicking back and forth in a *move it* gesture.

Wait...She was distracting him so I could attempt to get past him and to the door. If I could get through, I could lock him in here with Bee. He wouldn't hurt her. That much I was sure of, but it would give me time to alert Shem.

"I'm sorry, Bee," Michael said. "I need you to understand that this isn't personal."

I inched closer to him while his attention was on my friend.

"Of course, I know that," Bee continued. "You saved my life. You protected us. You're still protecting us, but you said you wanted to help fix the Morningstar. What changed? What did the Dominion offer you?"

He sighed. "The Dominion aren't my concern. I'll be dealing with them in due course."

"I don't understand," Bee pleaded. "Help me to understand."

I moved a little closer.

"The Dominion are hurting my people," Michael said. "Their greed is killing us, but I can change that. Once I deliver Shem's head, they'll give me my power back and then...then I'll use it to end them."

"You want to be in charge?" Bee's tone went up an octave in surprise.

"I can bring balance. I can bring harmony."

"By killing *all* the people in the mall?" She was starting to sound pissed off. Come on Bee. Keep your cool a little longer. Stroke the bastard's ego.

"Sacrifices must be made for the greater good," Michael said stiffly.

We were losing the arrogant, pompous wanker.

It was now or never. I clenched my fists and

dashed, ducking to slip past him and slamming into a wall of muscle.

"*Oompf.*"

He'd stepped into my path.

He gripped my shoulders hard enough to hurt. "Don't. Make. Me. Hurt. You."

"Let her go!" Bee attacked him, and the next moment I was free.

I hit the ground hard enough to jar my tailbone.

Bee fell on her side beside me, her head whipping up to glare at Michael with murder in her eyes. "You traitorous bastard."

Michael flinched. "I'm sorry that you feel that way." He made to turn away.

I scrambled toward him. "Wait!"

He paused.

"If you do this—if you kill Shem, there'll be no way back to heaven for you or your people. You'll be stranding yourself here. Is that what you want?"

"He doesn't want to go back. Do you?" Bee sneered.

"Heaven is now an unknown entity," Michael said. "The rules, the order...We won't fit there, but here we can make a home. The celestial energy production can be streamlined to be more humane." He turned to face us once more, his expression eager as if he was desperate for us to understand. "The Dominion keep humans caged, but it doesn't have to be that way. We can create a system where humans can live freely within the city walls and be happy to contribute to the production of celestial power."

I pulled myself to my feet alongside Bee. "Do you hear yourself? Free to live in the city walls? Walls! You want to keep us walled in and use us as batteries. And what about the fucking monsters? Hmmm?"

His expression closed off. "The monsters will die out eventually. Without humans to feast on, they'll turn on each other."

He'd thought this through. A new world order with him at the helm. He wanted power, and he was willing to betray us for it.

He strode toward the red door. "I'll be back for you both soon."

Bee and I rushed him, but he moved fast, slamming the door in our faces and locking it.

"Open this door!" Bee hammered on the metal. "Damn you, Michael." She clenched her teeth. "We fucked up. We fucked up bad. Oh shit. Gabriel..." She stared at me in dawning horror, and my stomach dropped.

"He must have told the Dominion Gabriel's plan."

"That's why he hasn't come." Bee closed her eyes, her mouth turning down. "That bastard. How did we not see it? How?"

"It doesn't matter now. We have to find a way to warn the others."

"And how do we do that from here?"

There had to be a way to get back into the mall, some...Wait a second... "Bee, do you still have the radio?"

"Fuck, yes!" She rummaged in her pocket to pull out the small walkie, hands shaking as she fumbled to depress the talk button. "Bee here, come in. Over."

Static.

"Hello? Bastian? Tumiel? Can you hear me? Over."

Nothing but static again.

"The reception is bad here," Bee said. "Shit."

I rattled the door again as if that would make a difference.

"Rue, what are we gonna do?" Bee asked.

We were separated from Bastian by layers of cement but... "If we can get to the tunnel above us, we might be able to get some reception."

"Isn't that area close to the runes tunnel?"

"Yes. But I think...I think it's also closer to the southern side where Bastian might be."

"Fuck." Bee took a deep breath. "Let's do this."

CHAPTER 13

BASTIAN

The motion detector lights turn on as I walk up and down the tunnel. Energy saving lights. Perfect for the job. We're almost done clearing out the route. Another day and it'll be ready for use. After that, we can scout the area above and make it as safe as possible by clearing out a building or two and prepping them as stop points on the way out of the city. We'll need non-perishables, blankets, and lanterns. General on-the-road supplies.

The fact that this route exists is no surprise. Jamie once showed me schematics he found of a town and its underground passages, as if the people who built the cities were afraid that humanity might one day need to hide from the sun.

Cities beneath cities, he'd called them. If the celestials hadn't come and helped us build our settlements, would humanity have been driven underground?

I'm hoping we never have to run from here, though.

I'm hoping that this place can become a home for many more humans for many years to come. Will the people here want to move to the Golden City after the monsters are gone? I doubt it.

"You've done good work," Tumiel says. "When the scout watcher team returns, we can get them to help clear out the rest of the tunnel."

"I can do it now."

"You need to rest." Tumiel looks at me with concern. "You look pale and tired."

Blunt as always. "I'm fine."

"Humor me, then."

I don't want to be reminded of my condition. I don't want to be seen as weak and dying. I have too much to do before that point, but he's right. I am tired. I could sleep. Waking up this morning was hard, and my limbs ache, but I'll be damned if I let anyone see my weakness.

I'll be damned if I give Rue anything more to worry about.

When I go, I'll do it quietly and quickly, hopefully in my sleep. "I'm fine. Let's get started and then—" My radio crackles.

"—astian...hear...trouble...Michael..."

I'd recognize Rue's voice anywhere even when overlayed with static. "Hello! Rue? Over."

"Thank God. Bastian you have to *crackle crackle.*"

"Rue? Rue? I can't hear you. You're breaking up. Over."

"Door *crackle* Michael *crackle* celestials *crackle* Fuck!"

Panic heats my blood. "Rue, where are you? Over."

The static starts and cuts off quickly, remains for longer, then cuts off again. A pattern.

Morse code!

"Bastian, what is it?" Tumiel asks.

"Hush." I hold up a hand to silence him and listen carefully to the intermittent static. The blood quickens in my veins as each word is deciphered.

The radio dies, and I break into a sprint.

RUE

The radio died as reception cut off. "Fuck!"

"It's okay," Bee said. "We gotta hope he got the Morse code message. Let's get back to the door."

We hurried through the tunnels, down a flight of steps and into the tube that led to the red door.

My chest fluttered with anxiety. What if Bastian

hadn't picked up on the code? What if he wasted time searching the mall for me? How much longer before the sentinels descended on this place?

Where the fuck was Michael?

The red door burst open, and Bastian stood in the frame looking like an avenging angel himself.

"Rue, what the fuck?" His eyes were wild as they went from me to Bee then back again.

"You got the message!" I threw myself at him and hugged him hard. He gave me a squeeze before pulling away. "We have to tell the watchers."

"Tumiel is on it."

"What are we going to do?" Bee asked.

"We're getting the hell out of here," Bastian said. "All of us. Now."

CHILDREN'S SCREAMS echoed off the walls as we took the broken escalators two steps at a time. People stood scattered around the central chamber, wide-eyed and frightened, their stunned focus on Shem beating the shit out of Michael.

His fist connected with the celestial's face again and again.

Michael took the punches, not bothering to fight back. He had what he wanted now, after all.

The upper hand.

"Enough!" Sarq grabbed hold of Shem. "He can't give us information if he's unconscious or dead."

Shem released Michael with a growl of disgust, and the celestial slumped to the ground, bloody and bruised. "How long?" Shem demanded. "How long do we have?"

Michael tucked his chin in. Mute and unresponsive.

"Damn you," Shem said. "I should never have trusted you."

There was no time for this. "We have to go. We have to get everyone out now." I clapped my hands to get everyone's attention. "Look at me. Hey! Eyes on me. Forget him. Grab your packs and meet at the southside door." The main route was known to Michael, but he didn't know about the second route. "Now. Move. All of you. Just one pack each. You have five minutes. GO!" Everyone scattered, galvanized by my orders. I turned to Bastian. "Get them out of here."

"We're not ready. The tunnel isn't clear."

"Then clear it as you go. Just go."

"You won't make it," Michael rasped. "It's too late."

I strode up to him and kicked him in the head. He toppled onto his side and looked up at me with bright blue eyes filled with sorrow. "You and Bee should have stayed in the tunnel, Rue. I was trying to save you, but now...Now you'll die too."

I'd trusted him, even grown to like him, even care about him a little, and he'd lied to us. "The only person that's dying today is you." I looked at Shem. "Kill him."

"No!" Bee rushed forward. "You can't..." She shook her head. "I mean...just leave him here. We can go."

"That's not you speaking, it's the fucking bond he made with you."

She pressed a fist to her chest and looked down at Michael with disgust. "Fuck."

A rumbling sound filled the chamber. "What is that?"

"They're here." Michael sat up and wiped at his bloody mouth. His face was already healing from Shem's attack. "Accept your fate, and it'll be quick and painless."

People ran past us, herded by Bastian and Zaq. We could do this. We had time.

Bastian ran over. "We need to go. Now."

The ground shook, and the ceiling began to crack.

Michael looked up. "They're here. Accept your fate calmly. There is no escape."

"Fuck you!" Bee snapped. "You...Argh!"

"We have to give the humans time to escape," Sarq said.

"There aren't enough of us to fight them," Penemue pointed out. "Baraqel and his team are out scouting."

"Your numbers, even with the scout team present, would be no match for the sentinel army." Michael stood slowly. "You're weak without celestial power. We will end you, and we will purge the humans. I've allowed you to vent your anger but no more." He held out his hand, and his sword appeared. "Now you will wait for judgment."

There was no time to waste. "Move! Everyone!"

We rushed after the stream of people headed for the southern exit. Zaq was up ahead ushering everyone through. "Follow Tumiel!" he ordered as they went past. "Keep going."

Bastian and Bee were ahead of us when a chunk of the ceiling came down between us. A cloud of dust filled the air, and blazing light sliced down over the rumble.

The celestials were here.

CHAPTER 14

"Rue!" Bastian attempted to double back, but Bee grabbed his arm.

"Go! I'll find you!" The light intensified. "Run!"

Shem grabbed me around the waist and hauled me away from the light. The next moment I was on the ground and the watchers' growls filled the air.

Someone tugged me to my feet and shoved me toward the escalators. "Run. Get out."

Sarq? "You can't fight them. They'll kill you."

His amber eyes filled with sadness. "We have to try. Now go!"

I grabbed his arm. "If Shem dies, we're all lost."

He cupped my face. "No. No we aren't, Rue, because you can do it. You can put it together too. He needs you to know that now." He pushed me again. "Go!"

Every fiber of my being wanted to stay. Every fiber wanted to search for Shem, to tell him how much I loved him. To hold him once more, but the world was in a chaos of streams of light and the slash of claws.

They were going to die. All the watchers were going to die unless...

Oh...Oh gods.

I knew what needed to be done.

I SLAMMED through the red door and into the tunnels, boots slapping on cement, then over metal grill and through the dark pipe leading to the ominous arch cordoned off by cones and painted with runes.

I stopped, doubling over, hands on my knees as I caught my breath.

What was I doing?

No. I had to do this.

It was the only way.

The celestials would kill my friends. My family.

Shem...

I had to save them.

This had to work.

I scuffed runes with my boots and wiped at them

with my hands, smudging them as much as I could because this had to disrupt their power, right? This had to stop them working.

The seconds ticked by, and my breath came faster, heart beating urgently. Come on. Come on.

A frisson of awareness raced over my skin, and the air was suddenly lighter.

Was this it? Had I disrupted the wards?

I stepped back, retreating to the tunnel that would lead me back to the red door and the mall.

The arch remained empty. I needed to call the devolved. Draw them out. A vise tightened around my chest and made it hard to breathe.

Focus, Rue. "Here goes nothing." I reached for the Morningstar power inside me, to the door that I'd finally learned to keep closed, gripped the handle, and yanked it wide open.

Power blasted through me. Hot. Potent. Filling my vision with light. My heart filled my chest, ribs aching with it.

I held it open for one, two, three—

Screeches filled the air, drifting from down the tunnel, and the loud scuttle of a multitude of limbs made the ground vibrate.

Hold it. Hold it, Rue.

One, two, thr—

The first devolved watcher appeared at the mouth

of the tunnel and slammed into the area where the runes began.

Once.

Twice.

Come on. My vision began to blur. I couldn't channel for much longer.

Three times now.

Several more creatures rushed forward to join the first.

They bashed the weakened wards.

Four.

Five.

Oh fuck, they were through.

They slowed, twitching and jerking as if they couldn't quite believe it, and then all eyes were on me.

I cut off the Morningstar power and ran.

BASTIAN

"Move. Everyone, keep moving."

I left her. I left her behind.

"It's not your fault," Bee says, telling me I've spoken out loud. "She'll be fine. Rue's a survivor, and she's with Shem, Sarq, and the other watchers."

But Amaros and Penemue aren't fighters. Tumiel and Zaq are, and they're here, with us. Herding the people. Here to protect them when they should be protecting Rue.

It's selfish. I know, but fuck it. "I have to go back."

Bee grabs me. "Stop it! Just stop! I know you love her, but you have to think logically. Even if you get to her, you can't help against the celestials. You'll be another body that needs protecting. Shem won't let any harm come to Rue."

"I should be the one comforting you."

"Yeah, you should, and you can when I fall apart later."

"Obstruction ahead. Everyone, all hands on deck!" Tumiel calls out.

I have to get out of here and find her. I can't lose her. We have time. I need that time.

RUE

There was no time to breathe as I sprinted through the tunnels with the devolved watchers on my tail. Don't look back. Don't fucking look back.

Scuttling, screeching, and wet, hungry sounds followed.

Hungry for me.

Hungry for the Morningstar power that clung to me.

But I'd give them a meal soon enough. I'd give them a buffet of celestials to chomp on.

I hit the stairs and barreled into the final tunnel where the red door loomed, propped open and ready for me to burst through.

My knee buckled, and I went down hard.

The monsters behind me cried out as if in triumphant joy.

I scrambled up and forward into a run, but I'd lost my distance advantage. They were gaining. I wasn't going to make it to the door.

A gust of air hit my back, a sign that something was close, leaping at me. Ready to snag me off my feet.

Icy terror flooded my limbs, and the next moment I was plucked off my boots, not by mandibles, but by muscular arms.

"I've got you," Kabiel said, running ahead of the devolved watchers with me clutched to his chest. "What were you thinking removing the runes?"

Relief left me weak and floppy in his arms. "The celestials are here. They're in the mall."

Kabiel growled. "Then we shall feast!"

CHAPTER 15

SHEM

Rue made it out.

She must have made it out.

Give me strength.

Give me the power to survive this. To find her once more.

I swipe at a celestial and duck to narrowly avoid his glowing blade. If I were at full strength, if my watchers were fueled, they wouldn't dare take us on.

We are warriors.

Front line fighters.

All these sentinels have are numbers and blades. But there are four of us against at least ten, maybe more. The bright light their weapons cast makes it hard to gauge their numbers accurately.

Amaros and Penemue are the scholars—the watchers of watchers—they're diplomats. But there is no room for diplomacy on the battlefield. They will fight, but their skills are rusty.

A blade's edge catches my shoulder, leaving a line of fire in its wake. Another slices at my cheek, then my calf.

I'm surrounded.

It's me they want.

I'm the threat.

The one that can bring back the Morningstar and send them all back to heaven.

"Shem!" Sarq shoves me and takes a blade to the shoulder.

His bellow of pain acts like a siren's cry to the celestials, who fall on us, eager to tear us to shreds.

I can't see Amaros or Penemue. For all I know, they're dead. But I spot Michael, standing on the periphery of the light, arms crossed, face in shadow.

There is no escaping.

There is no surviving this.

I'm sorry, Rue.

As the celestials close in to deliver their final blows, every hair on my body stands to attention.

Inhuman screams blast the air.

The celestials pull back, light dimming so that their horrified faces are visible.

"No!" Michael yells.

I twist my body away from them and see my heart cradled in a monster's arms.

"Shem!" Rue reaches for me, and Kabiel throws her at me, shouting at us to move.

I catch her neatly then fling myself out of the light and into the shadows.

There is no time to look back and watch as my devolved brethren decimate the celestials. No time to stop and bathe in their revelry as they feed fully for the first time in a decade.

The easiest route is blocked by rubble, so we take the eastern route. It's longer, but we can still get to the escape tunnel via it.

Sarq and I make it first, with Penemue close behind, Amaros hanging limply over his shoulder.

Around us, the mall creaks and cracks. The celestial invasion has weakened the structure. This whole place is about to collapse.

"We'll be safe in the tunnels," Sarq gasps out. He's losing blood, and his gait is wobbly.

"You're hurt!" Rue cries. "And Amaros…"

"We'll worry about healing once we're at a safe zone."

She presses herself to me, allowing me to carry her, and I know she's hurt too. She channeled to get the creatures to follow her. There's probably internal damage to her body. She'll need time to heal.

"This way!" Sarq shoves through a set of fire doors

into the corridor that leads down to the basement level and the new set of tunnels.

"Why didn't you tell me?" Rue asks. "Why hide that I can fix the Morningstar?" She shakes her head. "You told me you were the only one who could fix it. How did you manage to lie?"

"I didn't lie. I believed I was the only one who could fix it. But as time went on, I realized just how strong your connection with the Morningstar power is. You're more than a channel, Rue. You have direct access, and you can use that to bring the pieces together and allow the fragments to heal."

"But you didn't tell me."

"I hoped you'd never need to carry that burden. You had enough to worry about."

The lights flicker, and the ground shifts. I stop and brace myself, and Sarq lets out a warning cry.

"Fuck!" Penemue fumbles, trying not to lose his grip on an unconscious Amaros.

We're on the move again, a minute, no more, before a loud aching creak swells around us, followed by the sound of metal and joists bending. Then, with an almighty crack, the ceiling ahead of us comes crashing down.

Sarq backpedals, and we come to a halt as the dust cloud settles to reveal rubble and metal and no way forward.

"We're trapped," Penemue says. "We have to go back to the red door."

"We can't do that," Sarq says. "The devolved will tear us to shreds."

"Kabiel will—"

"Nothing. He can do nothing. They're in a feeding frenzy."

"And there is no way out for you." Michael's voice booms from behind us.

Rue goes stiff in my arms as I turn to face the bastard. "You're just as fucked as us, Micheal."

His smile is thin and smug. "No. I'm not. I have a calling Word." He holds up his hand, and his sword appears, glowing blue with the power of an extraction Word.

The highest-ranked warriors were given this power. A Word to pull them out of battle and to safety. The Dominion had given him one. "I can get out of here, and I can take one person with me." His attention drops to Rue, still cradled in my arms, and his mouth tightens. "Give me Rue. She doesn't have to die."

"Fuck you," Rue snarls. "I'd rather die than go anywhere with a traitorous bastard like you."

"You love her," he says to me. "You want her to live."

I need her to live. Aside from me, she's the only one who can save this world. She knows her worth isn't just to me, but to the fate of this world.

My grip on her slackens.

"No…" Rue looks up at me in horror. "What are you doing?"

I allow her to stand. "You have to go with him. I won't let you die here if there's a way that you can be saved." I look deeply into her eyes, hoping that she can read between the lines and understand what's truly at stake.

"No…" She scans my face. "No…"

I pull her into my arms and press my lips to her ear. "Hope is hidden in the church." I shove her away.

Her eyes are wide. She understands what I'm telling her, but in the next moment, her face crumples because she knows what this moment means. She shakes her head, eyes glistening with tears of frustration. "Fuck you, Shem." Her tone is soft. "Fuck you."

"I love you too."

She lets out a choked sob, and my heart squeezes painfully as I memorize her face. I want it to fill my mind in my final moments.

"Hurry," Michael snaps. "There's no time. Come." He holds out his hand.

Rue tears her gaze from my face and slowly turns to Michael.

His sapphire eyes brighten in triumph.

He thinks he's won.

He has no idea that he's taking hope with him, not ending it here.

She looks back at me one last time before holding

out her hand to Michael, but before Michael can grab it, a shadow bursts out from the wall and smashes into him.

He cries out in alarm and falls to the ground with the shadow on top of him.

Straddling him?

Michael lets out a shocked shout, then goes limp. The shadow figure slowly stands and turns to face us. Orange eyes gleam out of the darkness that makes up its face.

Rue backs into me, and I clutch her to me. What is this creature?

The screech of the devolved echoes down the corridor. They're coming for us.

The shadow expands then rushes toward us.

The world tips and goes dark. My knees buckle, and when they hit the ground, the lights come back on. I'm kneeling on hardwood with the sound of retching behind me.

"Shem..." Rue staggers toward me, wiping her mouth with the back of her hand. "What happened?"

Sarq is on his knees a little to my right, and Penemue is leaning over Amaros's prone form.

Shafts of sunlight lance through the air, dappling the ground. We're in some kind of store that's been gutted and boarded up. The ceiling is made up of dusty rafters and cobwebs, and the ground has patches of light and dark wood where units must have made up aisles.

I allow Rue to help me to my feet, and we stand, leaning against each other for a moment.

"The ghost…"

"That was no ghost," Sarq says.

"No." A female voice echoes around us. "I am no ghost."

My stomach clenches because I know that voice.

Rue has gone tense and still beside me. "Show yourself."

A figure materializes in front of us—slender, tall, and regal, with shimmering dark hair and eyes like fire.

"I know you," Rue says. "I…I think I dreamed about you. But I forgot and…Who are you?"

The woman looks at me and smiles. "Hello, Shemyaza. It's been a long time."

"Hello, Priyana, or should I call you Jilyana?"

CHAPTER 16

BASTIAN

We make it out of the tunnel just as the earth beneath our feet trembles.

"It's coming down!" someone cries. "It's all coming down."

Behind us, the mall shudders and sinks into the ground. It was already partially submerged, but now the whole thing has slipped into the earth.

"No!" Bee rushes forward. "No..."

I can't move. I can't fucking breathe. "She got out. She has to have gotten out."

"Yes," Bee says quickly. "She'll be fine. We just have to...We have to wait to rendezvous."

"Bastian, we need to move," Tumiel says. "We have

to find safe shelter before the sun sets."

I close my eyes and force down my panic. Rue is a survivor. She'll be fine. Shem has her. They're all fine. Probably on the other side of the city. "We need to head across the city. Find the others."

Tumiel nods. "There are a couple of buildings that might work as a shelter. Zaq scoped them out a month ago."

Drawn by the sound of his name, Zaq joins us. "A library and a bank."

"What's closest?" Bee asks.

"The library," Zaq says. "But the bank has shutters on the windows, and it's more secure."

We have maybe three hours before sunset. "Then we head for that."

Around us, people huddle together, staring at the remains of their home while the children cry.

"We might need to take a few minutes to calm everybody down," Bee points out.

As sympathetic as I am, my job now is to keep these people alive, not mollycoddle them. "Ten minutes, and then we move."

With Zaq scouting ahead, we make good time. Tumiel ends up carrying the boy, Sammy. The child has asthma and no medication. The dust and rubble seem to have aggravated his condition. He's limp and ashen in the watcher's arms. His mother, Clara, walks behind them, wringing her hands.

My gut tells me he won't make it if we can't get him some medication soon. "Keep an eye out for a pharmacy."

Bee nods. "Already on it."

"Great minds."

"Totally." She smiles, but the action is more reflex than anything else.

She's worried about Rue. About the watchers. About what this means for us. The mall was our sanctuary, and now it's gone.

What do we do from here? I have no fucking clue. These people...All these fucking people, and the only person I care about is Rue.

"There!" Bee points across the street at the green cross that signifies a pharmacy.

I jog ahead to join Tumiel. "We need to make a stop." I point across the street. "There might be medication in there."

"See the red cross painted on the ground outside the door?" Tumiel says.

"Yeah?"

"Means it's flagged as a no-go by the watcher scout team."

"There are monsters in there?"

"Maybe, or maybe they suspect there are."

Sammy's wheezing punctuates the silence, and Tumiel's mouth tightens. "Fuck."

Clara begins to cry.

The boy's airways are closing. If we don't act soon, they'll be too inflamed for us to get the medication into him. "We have to try. I can do it."

"I'm coming with you," Bee says. "I'm small. I can get into tight spaces if need be, and I'm a scout. We're trained to be quiet."

"Okay."

Tumiel looks torn, his emerald gaze fixed on Bee. "Any sign of occupation and you get out."

"Of course." She lifts her chin. "I don't plan on dying today."

His gaze softens. "Good."

Zaq doubles back. "All clear. The bank isn't far. A block away now."

"You keep moving," Bee says to Tumiel. "We'll find you. Go."

We jog across the street toward the boarded-up building. It's on the corner of a cluttered alley. The door is locked, but there's a window on the alley side. We manage to clear the debris of broken furniture and crates to get to it. The glass is long gone. It makes sense that something may have crawled in here and made it a home.

This is the only exit.

"We need to make another exit before we head in, just in case," Bee says.

"Agreed."

The windows are boarded up from the inside, and there's no getting the door open either.

There is only one entry point we can see, so only one exit. This is a bad idea.

Bee looks up at me, the conflict clear on her face. "That boy...Bastian, we have to do this."

I won't be able to live with myself if we walk away now. "We get in and we unlock that door."

"Good plan."

Bee climbs in first before I can protest. She's quick, small and light, but it takes me a little longer to get my frame through the window.

I'm no scout, but I'll do whatever it takes to protect Bee.

The inside of the pharmacy is dim and dusty, and most of the shelves are empty. There are planks of wood leaning up against the wall. I grab a slender one. A perfect weapon if needed.

A few packets of pills and sachets are scattered on the ground. Bee picks them up as we go, shoving whatever she finds into her pockets. We can examine it all later. We stay low and move quietly.

The front door is our first stop. It's locked and chained. No key.

Fuck.

There's no way to open it. Removing the boards will require a tool we don't have and even then, it would take forever, because it's obvious someone used a nail gun.

This is the point we should decide to leave.

Bee shakes her head and heads deeper into the shop.

The air smells like dust, peppermint, and something sharp and bitter. The scent is sharp and cloying when it hits my throat. I've never smelled anything like it before.

Bee comes to a halt at the end of an aisle and looks up at the large, curved mirror positioned high on the wall to allow a good view of the shop floor. There is no movement, just our shadowy figures crouched by the aisle.

The mirror doesn't show us what's beyond the counter.

She leans in close. "I'll go into the dispensary. You stay here. Run if you hear me scream." She empties out her pockets and hands me the sachets and pill packets.

"I'm not leaving you."

She glares at me. "I can move faster on my own. I can find a way out if I don't have to worry about you."

Ouch. I want to argue with her plan, but she's a scout, and this is what she does. My sweeper skills are useless without the serum or my blade. She's right. I'll be a liability to her escape, but I *can* fight to give her time to get out. She doesn't have to know that, though. So I nod. "Fine."

Satisfied, she dashes to the counter and slips beneath the hatch before vanishing into the dispensary beyond.

Five minutes. That's all I'm giving her.

Five minutes then I'll go after her.

My scalp prickles in awareness, and my gaze flies to the mirror, searching for movement. Nothing. I inch forward. There's a blind spot to the far right. An area of the shop floor not covered by this silver eye.

I need to check it out.

There can't be anything there because otherwise it would have spotted Bee when she crossed to the counter, but my body tells me differently.

My senses are in alert mode.

I need to check it out. I'm holding my breath as I peer around the end of the aisle, past the counter and into the shadows. Nothing moves.

There's nothing there.

But my gaze is drawn up the far wall, then up to the ceiling. My heart stutters.

A large mass clings to the cracked plaster. Veiny and dark crimson, it pulses slowly like a heartbeat.

It shudders suddenly and pushes out at one end as if...Oh fuck. There's something inside it.

There's something inside, and it's trying to get out.

CHAPTER 17

RUE

Jilyana was the woman from the dreams that I'd had while in the Golden City. The details were fuzzy, but her face, not that I saw it, was familiar.

This was the djinn who'd betrayed Shem. He'd believed her to be human and fallen in love with her. But before that...before *any* of that, she'd been in love with Michael. The celestial had handed her over to the Dominion when he discovered her true nature. He'd betrayed her for his duty. For power, no doubt, just as he betrayed us. A pattern I should have considered, but he'd fooled me completely.

Had he fooled Jilyana too? Lured her into a trap and handed her over to the Dominion? The way she'd attacked him at the mall...There was rage there and justifiably so.

She stared at me, her amber eyes scrutinizing me as if searching for something.

Shem placed himself between us, shielding me with his body so that I had to peer around his bicep to see her.

She was tall and regal, emanating power. I should have been afraid, but I wasn't. "You were in my dream."

She smiled at me. "You remember."

"Don't look at her!" Shem snapped at Jilyana. "You speak only to me."

Jilyana's smile fell. "You were always so protective, Shemyaza." Her gaze flicked back to me. "But you have no cause to worry. I mean your human no harm."

"I don't believe you," Shem replied.

"Liar," she said. "You know I speak the truth."

His jaw clenched. "I don't know anything about you. Everything I believed to be true was proven to be a lie. You lied to me, and I failed to hear it."

Her throat bobbed. "I'm sorry. If I'd had a choice... It matters not. What is done is done. We must move forward."

"You can start by explaining how you got into the mall," Sarq said.

"I followed Rue," she replied. "Once she helped me escape the Golden City."

"What?" Shem looked from me to Jilyana.

What was she talking about. "I didn't help her escape. I...I didn't..."

"Yes, you did," Jilyana said. "Although you probably don't recall it. It will come back to you now that I exist fully on this plane."

An image flashed in my mind. A small square room with no windows or doors, every inch of wall, floor, and ceiling covered in runes. The dream...She'd been trapped there. "They had you trapped inside a cage of runes."

"Not my first prison, but certainly my most elaborate. The Dominion held me captive one way or another for decades. You see, the divine light closed off the doorway to my world a long time ago, but there was a window through which some of us were able to pass. I spent much time among humans, playing at being human. I enjoyed their company. I met Michael during one of my sojourns. He was playing human too. We fell in love...at least I thought we did, but when I shared my truth with him, he revealed his identity and betrayed me. He gave me to the Dominion. They should have passed me to the higher echelon to send me home, I know that now, but they kept me. They told me lies. They set conditions for my return."

"They asked you to trick Shem."

"Yes. They asked me to make him fall in love with me. To trust me and open his heart and mind to me so that I could possess him. They told me that destroying the Morningstar was the *only* way for me to go home. The only way to open the doorways kept locked by the divine being."

Open some doorways for sure. The bastards.

"And you believed them?" Shem asked incredulously.

"Yes. I did. And when it was all said and done, they did not send me home."

"Of course they didn't," Sarq sneered. "The doors to the djinn realm are sealed by God himself. Only he can open them."

Something about her story wasn't clicking. "The Dominion couldn't send you back to your world, but why did they have you locked away in a room covered in runes? Why not just let you go?"

Her eyes were pools of sadness. "Because when the Morningstar shattered...when the fragments were propelled out of their haven and into this world, one fragment made its home inside me."

It took a moment to register what she was saying, but then...then it all made perfect sense. "*You're* the relic that Kabiel saw."

"Bullshit," Shem said. "I'd feel it if a relic was near."

"Would you?" Jilyana arched a brow and then a prickle ran over my skin—power, hot, insistent, and as familiar as the Morningstar energy that I channeled.

It cut off abruptly after a moment.

Shem sucked in a sharp breath. "Shit."

Jilyana sighed. "I can mask it if I wish, but it allowed me to sense you," she said to me. "I managed to connect with you when you were asleep and draw you to me. I felt the Morningstar power. Your being close allowed me to build a bridge between us, and I was able to use it to escape from my prison."

Flashes of memory flitted through my mind. The fight with the crabine, being knocked unconscious, then... "You forced your way into my head...Into my body!"

Shem's chest rumbled. "You *invaded* her?"

Her brows came down in a frown. "I saved your life. And again today."

She had a point. "You did. And you're here. You have the relic piece. It means...It means we're almost done."

"Give it to me," Shem demanded.

She took a breath and looked him dead in the eyes. "I can't."

"What? Why not?"

"Because it's a part of me now. The only way to extract it is to bring me to the other three pieces. Once that happens, it'll be drawn out of my body."

Then that's what we'll do. "You saved my life twice. Once to save your own, but the second time...You didn't have to do that."

Her mouth turns down. "Anything to see that bastard Michael fail."

Shem made a sound of agreement.

I stepped around him to face her, and this time he didn't stop me. "You're part of our team now, Jilyana, which means no secrets and no lies."

She looked at Shem when she spoke. "Never again. I swear it."

I felt Shem relax behind me. "I believe you."

Shem could sniff out a lie easily, and yet she'd tricked him into believing that she loved him...unless... Unless her love for him hadn't been a lie at all.

SARQ HAD HEALED and Amaros was healing too, but slowly. Too slowly. We were a mere hour away from sundown, and this building wasn't a secure place to stay the night.

"I can channel and heal him."

"No. You've channeled enough today," Shem said. "You've probably done internal damage. You need to heal."

"I can help him," Jilyana said. "I can speed up his healing."

"Please." Penemue looked up at her with red-rimmed eyes. "Please save him."

It hit me that throughout our whole interaction with Jilyana, Penemue hadn't said a word. His whole focus, every iota of his attention had been on Amaros, and now...Now that look in his eyes was as if his whole world was crashing down.

He loved him. It was as clear as day to me now.

"Do it," Shem said.

Jilyana crouched beside Amaros and gently placed her hands over the wound on his abdomen. A soft, golden glow spread from the point of contact, and after a moment, she removed her hands. The wound had healed.

"Amaros?" Penemue said. "Can you hear me?"

Amaros groaned and opened his eyes. "Pen?"

Penemue let out a sob of relief. "You're fine. You'll be fine."

"Can you stand?" Sarq asked.

He groaned and sat up slowly. "I think...I think so."

"Good because we have to move."

Shem was by the boarded-up window, looking out. "I know where we are. South of the mall. Not far from the city limits."

I joined him at the window, slipping between his body and the sill to look out.

He placed his hands on my hips, anchoring me to him.

There was a hair salon across the street and farther down from that a supermarket, then a pharmacy.

"There's a library we can bunk in," Sarq said. "It's close."

Penemue helped Amaros up and braced him with an arm around his waist. "Let's move."

"What about the others?" I looked up at Shem. "Where would they have come out?"

"Not far from here," Shem said. "We can search for them in the morning. There's no way of finding them now."

But there was. I had a method in my pocket.

I pulled out the radio. If Bastian or Tumiel still had theirs, then we could contact them.

There'd been no reception in the tunnels, but up here, there should be no interference.

I depressed the button. "Bastian, it's Rue, can you hear me? Over."

CHAPTER 18

BEE

I can't believe what I'm seeing here. Antibiotics and antiseptic cream. Tubes and powder and sterile liquid in vials. Most of it will be out of date, but we learned a long time ago that even the expired stuff has some benefits.

This place is untouched. I'm tempted to load up, but I need to find the inhalers first. The boy will need steroids to open his airways. A few moments of rummaging, and I find the inhalers. There are a bunch. I grab a few and shove them in my pockets.

I need a bag for the rest, and I find one shoved between a desk and the wall. I empty out the contents —a plastic lunch box, a thermos, and a battered book. Two minutes later, the bag is bulging with supplies.

My pulse pounds with excitement. This is amazing. A true haul. The kind of haul that we rarely got back when we were scouting for the settlement.

It feels like such a long time ago when it's only been a matter of weeks.

There's a door at the back of the room. More medication? More supplies? The handle pushes down easily. It's not locked. The room beyond is dark, and the strange sharp smell from the main floor is stronger here, as if it's originating from this room.

It takes a moment for my eyes to adjust and make out shapes: a desk, a coat rack, a chair shoved against the wall, and...what...What is that?

The large misshapen thing moves up and down. Slow and even movements like...like breathing.

My vision adjusts further, and ice pricks my scalp because there's a monster in the corner of the room.

It hasn't seen me. It's curled away from me with its face toward the wall.

Sleeping?

Probably.

I back up and slowly, carefully, close the door.

I'm slick with cold sweat as I hurry out of the dispensary and into the main store.

Bastian is at the counter looking like he's about to leap over it. He steps back quickly as I emerge.

"We have to go. Now." His voice is barely a whisper,

but I'm adept at lip reading. We had to do it a lot as scouts.

I pass him the heavy pack, then quickly climb over the counter. He grabs my arm and points to the ceiling where a huge crimson sac is pulsing.

"Monster in back room," I whisper.

He nods, and we head for the exit.

If there's one monster and an egg sac, then there could be more of them close by. Most monsters hunt at night, but that doesn't mean they can't be awake in the day. There could be more on their way here right now, and there's something else...Another issue niggling at the back of my mind that I can't quite grasp.

We're a few feet from the window when loud static fills the air and a voice cuts through the silence.

"Bastian, it's Rue, can you hear me? Over."

Bastian's eyes fly wide open because the sound is too loud. My already pounding pulse begins to race. Bastian fumbles with the radio, trying to get it out of his pocket and shut it off while my eyes dart around the store from shadow to shadow, aisle to aisle looking for movement because my senses are in alert mode.

Something is coming.

The monster from the back room.

We're at the window when he finally frees the radio from his pocket.

"Bastian, come in. Over."

Fuck, fuck, fuck.

The static dies as he turns the radio off. His gaze comes up and over my head, and his face freezes in shock.

Fingers of ice grip my nape, forcing my head to turn. Forcing me to look over my shoulder at the huge monstrous shape standing at the other end of the room.

It looks like a large misshapen dog but with front legs that look like arms...Oh shit. I know what this is.

Herald's claw.

And it's staring right at us.

RUE

I shoved the radio into my pocket. "Dammit. Nothing."

"There's something out there," Shem said. "Movement on the roof of the pharmacy."

I pressed close to the window again, peering through the gaps in the planks, and caught site of a dark shape.

Wait... "Is that—"

"Herald's claw," Shem confirmed. "This is odd. They don't emerge during the day unless disturbed."

"It's close to sundown," Sarq said.

"We can't leave now," Shem said. "Dammit."

We were about to back away from the window when a couple of figures ran out of the alley at the side of the building.

Bastian and Bee.

And hot on their tail was a second herald's claw.

My heart slammed into my rib cage. "Fuck!" I tore away from Shem and ran for the door.

He grabbed my arm. "Not you. You stay."

As much as it grated, he was right. I had no weapon. I was useless up against a claw. "Fine, but hurry."

He and Sarq beelined for the exit, and I headed for the window again.

Bastian and Bee stood back-to-back while the two herald's claws circled.

"That's strange," Penemue said. "They should have attacked by now."

But it looked like they were sniffing the air.

"Oh..." Penemue said. "They can smell death."

Bastian...They knew he was dying.

Shem and Sarq appeared in the street running toward the beasts. Both watchers took to the air and attacked.

My heart thrummed in my throat as Sarq and Shem fought the creatures.

Bastian grabbed Bee and pulled her out of the way.

They ran out of sight, and a moment later my radio crackled. "Rue, where are you? Over."

Relief at hearing his voice made my throat tight. "Store across the street from you." I hurried to the exit. "Boarded-up windows." I stepped outside and waved to get their attention.

The growls and snarls of the fight were louder in the street, and my pulse quickened in response. Bastian and Bee spotted me and ran over, but there was no time for a reunion because more claws had appeared on the rooftops.

Three more. Oh shit.

One of them leapt into the fray, aiming for an airborne Shem.

"Shem, watch out!"

Shem went down beneath the creature.

"No!"

A blast of heat hit my back, and the next moment Jilyana was running toward the creatures. Flames shot out of her hands and lit up the claw on top of Shem.

It howled and rolled off him. Another jet took out a second claw. Jilyana buckled and fell to her knees.

I made a break for her, and Bastian tried to grab me, but I evaded, legs pumping as I closed the distance between myself and the djinn.

"I got you. Come on."

She grabbed my arm. "There are more coming. We have to help. Together." She looked up at me with fire dancing in her eyes.

I tore my gaze away and up to the rooftops where

several more herald's claw had appeared. Shem and Sarq had taken out four of them, but they were flagging.

"What can we do?"

"Channel through me," she said.

"What?"

"Push the power through me; the relic fragment will focus it. We can kill them. Together."

I didn't know that was a possibility, but I trusted this woman. "Okay, what do I do?"

"Take my hand."

I grasped it and pulled her to her feet. My palm tingled with the evidence of her power.

"Do it. Now."

I opened the door inside me, jerking as the power flooded me, rushing down my arm and into Jilyana. She pushed out her free hand and pointed at a herald's claw. A javelin of dark energy shot out and slammed into the claw. It lit up white and glowing, then disintegrated. She pointed at a second, and a third, taking them out one by one, somehow turning the Morningstar power into a weapon.

My chest ached, heart expanding as a burning lit up inside me. "I can't...I can't hold it much longer."

"Just a moment more." She took out another claw.

There were still three left. I had to hold on. I had to—

Battle cries filtered past the rush of blood in my

head, and a moment later, Baraqel and his team barreled into the fray. The fresh wave of watchers tipped the balance in our favor.

I slammed the door shut, sagging on my feet and gasping for air as the last of the claws were torn to shreds.

The fight was over in seconds, but if not for Jilyana, Shem and Sarq would have been overwhelmed.

Shem wiped blood off his face and strode over to join us, his gaze equal parts wary and speculative as they raked over Jilyana and me. "We'll discuss this when we're in a safe place."

"The bank," Bastian said, joining us. "Everyone is at the bank."

"In that case, lead the way." Shem looked down at my hand in Jilyana's. "You can let go of her now," he said to the djinn.

She released me and ducked her head, but I caught the hurt on her face before she did, and annoyance flitted in my chest. She'd hurt him, lied to him, and tricked him, yes, I understood that, but she'd been used herself. All she wanted was to go home, and instead she'd been held captive for decades. What she'd done was wrong, but she was trying to atone.

"Thank you, Jilyana. Thank you for saving our lives."

She looked up at me in surprise. "You're most welcome."

Bastian pulled me into a hug, squeezing me tight. "I was so fucking worried about you."

I hugged him back, tension draining out of my limbs. "I was worried about you when I saw you out here with the claws. You and Bee both..." I closed my eyes and reveled in the contact. He was safe. We'd made it out.

He broke the hug and tucked me against his side, then looked over at Shem. "Okay, now we can get going."

"Let's move," Shem said.

The watchers flanked us as we set off down the street, and after a few moments Shem fell into step beside us. "Don't get too close to Jilyana, either of you. Don't give your trust so easily. Promise me you'll be careful around her."

I glanced over my shoulder at Jilyana, who looked suddenly lost and adrift, and couldn't help the twinge of empathy that filled me. But was it real? Or was she somehow putting it there? She'd been in my body, in my head...Shem was right. I needed to be wary.

Because with Jilyana, I was literally playing with fire.

CHAPTER 19

The bank was a safe spot where we were able to pull down metal shutters to keep out the monsters. The watchers scoped out the building before we settled on the ground floor in the main room. It was a bare space with a checkout counter running along the back. A thick plastic window extended from the counter up to the ceiling. People would have stood behind that counter to serve customers with the plastic as a barrier.

I'd seen such scenes in movies that had survived the decimation of the old world.

Money had mattered back then. Paper and silver and gold. Now the only currency that mattered was skill. Trade and barter were our way. Precious metals and gems meant nothing.

It wasn't late, but everyone was exhausted. Sleep

came quickly, even without the comfort of bedding or blankets, because in this shitty world, sleep brought the comfort of oblivion, taking us away from reality for a little while.

Sleep was a reprieve that we all craved, but I doubted it would find me easily tonight.

Instead, I watched over our people as they huddled in clusters on the threadbare brown carpet, pillowing their hands on backpacks and each other as they slipped into dreams to forget the horror of what had happened and the uncertainty of what was to come.

Bastian slipped his arms around me from behind and drew me against his chest. "We'll be safe here tonight. It's secure."

I leaned into his body, allowing him to support me for a moment. "Good. Because everyone is exhausted. The shock of the last few hours has hit."

He kissed the top of my head. "But we're alive. Which means we get more time."

Bee approached looking apologetic. "Hate to break up the hugfest, but Shem wants us in the side room."

Yeah, business. We had plenty to attend to.

"How's Sammy?" Bastian asked her.

"Better. The meds are working. It'll be a day or so before he's back to normal, but he's breathing easier now."

"Worth it, then."

"Totally."

The haul of meds they'd brought back with them would be invaluable on the road ahead.

Shem appeared in the doorway to the interview room. His gaze zeroed in on me, and a jolt of awareness shot through me.

I'd been summoned.

We joined the watchers in a side room, probably used for interviews or something back when the world was normal.

Normal…What was that, anyway? This…this was normal now.

There were a couple of filing cabinets shoved against a wall and a small window high up that had been boarded over haphazardly.

Jilyana sat on a plastic chair in a corner looking warily at the watchers, some of whom were making no secret of how disgusted they were to have her with us.

She was an athletic-looking female, but she seemed to have shrunk, surrounded by these hulking watchers.

Baraqel stared right at her, his top lip up in a silent snarl, and she quickly ducked her head as if expecting to be struck.

Indignant rage burst in my chest. "Stop it." I stepped in front of her. "All of you, fucking stop looking at her like you want to hurt her."

"She's the reason we're in this mess," Baraqel snarled.

With his tusks, angry scarlet skin, and stocky tank build, Baraqel could be a frightening sight, but I wasn't afraid of him or any of the watchers. Right now, I was pissed.

I held his glare defiantly. "The *Dominion* are the reason. Jilyana was merely a pawn. She saved our lives back at the mall, and she saved mine outside the Golden City. If she hadn't helped with the herald's claw, then Shem and Sarq might be dead. She deserves a second chance."

"*You* don't get to decide that," Baraqel snapped.

"Enough!" Shem growled, low and menacing. "Moderate your tone when you speak to her."

"Really?" Baraqel said. "You'd make the same *mistake* twice?" He flicked a glance Jilyana's way.

"What is your fucking problem?" Bee asked him.

Baraqel made to turn on her, but Tumiel stepped forward, baring his teeth in warning.

Bee arched a brow and crossed her arms as if to say, *Take that, bitch.*

Baraqel looked from Bee to Tumiel then back again. "You're all insane." His tone held no heat now. In fact, he sounded tired, as if this whole deal had become too much. "Trust the djinn if you want. I, for one, will reserve my judgment."

He didn't get it. "This isn't about trust. It's about decency. If Jilyana betrays us, then trust me, I'll be the last person standing in her corner. But until then, we put away the fangs and the claws, okay?"

Baraqel snorted softly. "I see Shem's been training you in pretty words."

"What we need now is shelter," Penemue said, blatantly changing the subject. "Somewhere the humans can stay while we go find the final piece of the relic."

"We don't even know where the final piece is," one of Baraqel's scouts said.

Kabiel would have known, but Kabiel was probably dead. He'd saved my life and paid for it with his own.

I was sick of having to be saved. I wanted to be the one doing the saving. Kabiel's sacrifice couldn't be in vain. "We'll have to try to locate it using the Morningstar power."

"Which could take weeks," Baraqel said.

"Which is why we need to find somewhere for the humans," Penemue reiterated. "Somewhere close. The longer we travel with them, the more of them we're likely to lose."

Baraqel lifted his chin. "My troop and I will protect them."

"We can't leave you in the city, though," Tumiel replied. "It's too dangerous."

"We'll all have to go," Shem said. "They'll be safe at location twelve."

Twelve? That rang a bell. Wait, that was the church

where the relics were hidden. The same church where Shem and I had first...yeah. That zone was safe because the celestials and monsters avoided it or didn't seem to see it. "Twelve will be safe once we get there, but the journey won't be."

Shem fixed his startling blue gaze on me. "We don't have a choice."

Silence claimed the room for long seconds.

"How far is it?" Jilyana asked finally.

Zaq replied, "A day by air, but more like three by foot. Maybe longer, depending on how fast the humans walk."

"I might be able to transport a small group of people," she said. "But I'd need at least a day to get my energy levels up. And once I'm there, I won't be able to port for a while. The distance and exertion will deplete me."

"That's fine," Shem said. "We just need you to make the one trip."

"Is it safe to wait a day?" one of Baraqel's troop asked. "Won't the Dominion send sentinels to find out what happened to the first troop?"

"They will," Shem said. "But I think waiting a day would be in our favor. Let them scour from above. They won't risk landing to investigate deeper. They'll see nothing, and they'll leave."

"We can send the children with you," Penemue said to her. "And some adults to watch over them."

"And you and Amaros," Shem added, looking to Jilyana to check if that was all right.

She smiled tentatively. "I can manage that."

"And the rest?" Zaq asked.

Baraqel made a soft sound of annoyance. "If we could find a vehicle with gas in the tank..."

"What about bicycles?" Bee suggested. "Is there a bike store in the city?"

"We need a map of the city so we can check," Bastian said.

"Wait a second..." Bee rushed out of the room and returned a moment later with a small booklet in a plastic pouch. "They have a tourism rack. This is a map of the city."

She spread it out over the table, and we scanned it, looking for a bike store.

"Here!" Bastian said. "We can go there once the sun comes up. It's not far. Two or three trips and we can bring back enough bikes for us all."

"Not everyone can ride, though." Bee gnawed on her lip. "We'll need to teach them. It shouldn't take more than a day."

We'd had a few bicycles in the settlement—novelty pieces, really. As scouts we'd attempted to use them for a little while, but a bike's speed had nothing on a ripper.

"The bicycles will work for part of the journey,"

Shem said. "But there is a stretch where they won't be able to go."

"I can plot an alternate route," Zaq said. "It would take longer on foot, but with the bikes…"

"The celestials will be on aerial lookout too," Penemue pointed out. "We'll need to be wary."

Baraqel growled. "Let those bastards come. We'll tear them to shreds. The devolved aren't the only ones who can have bloodlust. They had the pleasure of killing the traitor Michael and his sentinels, but we'll take the pleasure of annihilating the next troop that descends on us."

"Unless that troop happens to be Powers," Amaros said softly. "We can't let anger get the best of us."

"We don't know if Michael is dead," Shem said. "He had an escape Word. He could have ported out before the mall collapsed."

The mood darkened. "If he is alive, then he'll come for us."

"And if he does, then we will deal with him," Sarq replied. "But for now, our focus must be on getting the humans to safe zone twelve."

"Everyone, get some rest," Shem said. "We're going to need it."

CHAPTER 20

The watchers left the interview room, but Shem remained, his palms on the table, head bowed. He looked defeated.

I hated that.

I wrapped my arms around his waist from behind and laid my cheek on his back. "We'll figure this out. We'll finish it. I promise."

He covered my hand with his. "I know." He turned to face me and pulled me into a hug. "I know."

I leaned into him, and for a moment it felt like it was just the two of us in the room.

"The main room is full. We should bunk in here," Bastian said finally.

Shem nodded. "Yes. I need to do a perimeter check."

"I'll come with you," Bastian said.

The two left, and I found a spot on the carpet where I could lean up against the wall.

"You look wiped," Bee said, lowering herself onto the floor next to me.

"I feel it."

Her gaze flicked to Jilyana, still sitting on the chair, her attention on the door. There was a deep sorrow to her expression. A sense of discomfort and displacement. As if she wasn't sure she should be here.

The woman had been held captive in a magical cube for goodness knew how long. This...this must be so strange for her, and being treated like a pariah didn't help.

"Jilyana, it won't always be like this, you know. With them. They'll realize you're not the enemy soon enough."

Her smile was watery and lost. "I don't blame them for hating me. *I* hate me."

"Yeah, I get it. It'll take time for you to get over that. We can't change the past, but we can fix the here and now. We can prepare for a better future."

"I'll do whatever it takes to make this right. This world...I suppose it's my home now."

"I'm sure there's a way to get you back to your world if you want. Once we've dealt with the monsters and the celestials, we'll find it."

A smile bloomed in her eyes. "I can see why he loves you."

Shem had said he loved me in the mall. *I love you too*...Said in response to me telling him to fuck himself. It could be construed as sarcasm, but the tone...the tone had been all too real. He'd said it and meant it because he'd believed it was the last chance to do so. He loved me, and that was enough. I wouldn't push him to hear those words again because we had a world to fix, and that...that had to come first.

THE NIGHT FELT like it dragged on, and even though I slept and rested, my body disagreed. I woke at dawn, warm and cozy, sandwiched between Shem and Bastian. Shem's arm was slung over my hip, his face tucked against my nape, and Bastian lay facing me, one arm tucked under his head and the free hand holding mine. They breathed in unison—deep and even—and I lay still for long seconds reveling in this moment with them.

I'd found bliss in a time of uncertainty, and I wanted to hold on to it for as long as possible.

There was enough light streaming in from between the boards on the window for me to make out the shapes in the room. The other watchers lay around us, and the top of Bee's golden head nestled on Tumiel's chest.

But where was Jilyana?

Ah, there she was, on the other side of the room, curled up in a ball. Alone. She must be cold. I tried to slip free of the guys, but Shem's grip on me tightened, and Bastian groaned softly in protest.

"Rue?" Shem's warm breath kissed my skin. "Go back to sleep."

I relaxed. "I was going to check on Jilyana. She's in the corner. She must be cold."

"She's djinn," Shem said as if that was explanation enough.

"So?"

"They don't feel cold. Or hot. Or...anything like that."

"They don't?"

"They're elemental beings, and they experience the world differently than humans, just as celestials do."

"Well, thank you for keeping me warm."

He nuzzled the spot below my ear. "Hmmm, pleasure."

"Is it morning?" Bastian mumbled, his eyes still closed.

"Yes," Shem said. "Go make coffee."

Bastian snorted. "Fuck you, Shem. You make it."

"I don't think we have any coffee...do we?" Ah, hope, the fickle bitch.

"Mira has some," Zaq piped up from somewhere in the room.

"I do," Mira replied groggily. "Never go anywhere without it."

I couldn't help the smile that bloomed on my face because we might be in a shitty situation right now, but we were together, and we had the promise of coffee.

I'd call that a win.

EVEN COFFEE COULDN'T CHASE AWAY the stiffness in my limbs.

"You channeled too much," Shem said. "You need to rest and heal. You'll stay here with Jilyana while we go and get the bikes." It was an order, and I didn't argue.

I'd be a liability out there today. "I'll help Mira rustle up a meal with the rations everyone has."

He stroked my cheek with his fingertips. "Then rest. Promise me."

I leaned into his touch. "I promise."

Bastian, Bee, Shem, and his troop left a few minutes later. The store was two blocks away, so it wouldn't take them long to get there and back, but I couldn't help the sense of unease that crawled over my skin.

The celestials would be looking for us. If Michael had gotten away, he wouldn't let up until he found us.

The watchers had chosen the city as a hideout because it was crawling with monsters, which kept the celestials at bay, but they'd come yesterday because they'd known our location for certain. They'd come again when their troops failed to return.

They'd come for Shem.

And he was out there right now, in plain sight.

I clenched my fists and forced myself to take a breath. The sooner we got out of the city, the better.

CHAPTER 21

SHEM

We're almost at the bicycle store when I sense a presence of celestials. Luckily, we're undercover of an awning.

"We have aerial surveillance," Tumiel says.

We all step deeper into the shadows and wait. Zaq is up ahead somewhere, and I can only hope he's hidden.

Long minutes pass, and the tingle across my scalp doesn't let up.

"They won't land unless they see a reason to," Sarq says softly, as if to reassure himself.

We wait in silence for several more minutes before

the tension in the air ebbs and the sound of beating wings grows distant.

"They'll circle back. They'll keep looking," Tumiel says. "We need to move fast and stay in the shadows or between the buildings.

"We won't be able to hide on the way back," Bastian points out. "We'll have bikes with us."

Fuck, he's right. "Let's get there and see what they have. All we need to do is confirm there are bikes that we can use. We need maybe two to take back with us so that those who can't ride can learn. The celestials will sweep the city today, and if they find nothing, then hopefully they'll move on."

"Michael knows that we're alive," Sarq points out. "If he made it out, he won't give up."

"He has no idea where Jilyana transported us. He'll widen the net." We're going to be in danger up until the moment we get to the church, there's no way around that. All we can do is be vigilant.

We make it to the store a few minutes later. Zaq is crouched outside the building. The huge windows on the store are smashed, and glass litters the pavement, but there are machines visible inside, rows and rows of gleaming bikes.

"Yes!" Bee says.

We cross the road quickly and duck inside, careful of any shards still clinging to the frames.

Bastian begins examining the bikes. "It's been a long time," he mutters.

Zaq heads deeper into the building, following his instinct to scope out the place for threats. He vanishes into the gloom, but I'm not worried. He can handle himself.

"This one is a good size for a child." Bee pulls out a small bike.

"The children will go with Jilyana," Sarq says.

We have one day for her to rest, and it might not be enough for her to recharge, despite what she said to me. "Take it anyway, just in case she isn't able to do the transport."

Bee picks out a bike fit for a child, and Bastian chooses an adult-sized one just as Zaq comes rushing into the room, eyes bright with excitement.

"I found something."

We follow him down a short hallway and through a door into a large garage space, and in the center of the garage sits a bus.

Bastian sucks in a sharp breath.

This could be the solution to our problem. "Bastian...can it work?"

"I just need...I need to check the engine and the fuel tank."

I have no idea what he's doing, but it takes a while of prodding and probing before he looks up with a grin. "It's a modified engine."

"What does that mean?"

"It means it's able to run on various fuel."

"Like kerosene?" Bee points to several containers in a corner marked *Kerosene*.

Bastian's eyes are alight with excitement. "Yes, like kerosene."

He wipes his hands on his jeans, a fresh smile tugging at his lips. "We have a vehicle."

With the contraption as transport, we might just get all the humans to safety after all, but something inside me remains wary, a soft vibration that spawns a dark foreboding inside me, because if Michael is still alive, then no one is safe until I hold the complete Morningstar in my hands.

All I can do is hope that he didn't make it out of the mall alive.

CHAPTER 22

MICHAEL

The Dominion finish probing my mind, and I slump to the ground, my body trembling from the residue of their power. I'm so weak I can barely lift my head. It's taken everything I have to bury my true intention deep in my psyche in a place that they can't find it.

"You failed, Michael," they say in that booming way of theirs.

I'm usually cowed by the magnitude of their presence, but not today. My body may be weak, but there is fire in my belly. Rage and indignation burn bright within me.

I won't be blamed again.

I won't be silent. "I didn't fail. You did. You failed to

tell me about Jilyana. You failed to tell me that you had her locked away here, that she holds the relic piece inside her." I felt the power of the relic before she forced me into unconsciousness.

It wasn't hard to connect the dots and realize that she is what Kabiel saw in his vision.

The relic hidden in the Golden City.

A prisoner.

Guilt attempts to grapple hold of my mind, but I fight it off.

Her fate is not my fault. "I did what you asked. I gained Shem's trust, and I summoned the sentinels. It is no fault of mine that they were overwhelmed by the devolved watchers." I don't bother to modulate my tone. "You want me to bring you Shemyaza's head, but you refuse to give me the tools to do so. This is your fault, and if he succeeds in his mission, that too will be on you."

Silence, heavy and ominous, presses in on me.

I have nothing to lose. If they smite me now, then so be it, but I know deep in my gut that they won't do that. They need me. I'm the only celestial who can match Shemyaza when he is at full power which, if he gets the Morningstar fragments, he will be.

So I push. "You promised to restore me to power if I brought you Shemyaza's head. But I cannot complete this task without the power. Make me whole now and I can give you what you want. I can stop the Morningstar being reassembled. This world is our home now, and I will *not* be torn from it."

"It seems that we have underestimated your loyalty once again, Michael. You're correct. Time is running short. Gabriel and his sympathizers have escaped."

Ice crystallizes in my lungs. "What?"

"We cannot expend resources to find them. Our focus must remain on the Morningstar and on Shem and...there is more..." The tension in the air spikes, and I wait. "There is more to the Morningstar than anyone knows. Something that we discovered a long time ago, and if you are to succeed in your mission, then you must be made aware of it also. Once you know the truth, there is no turning back. We will restore you. Make you our champion. Our voice. Our hand. But once you claim this honor, there is no turning back. Do you want it?"

Maybe there is no need to betray them. No need to take the helm when I can steer the ship regardless. "Yes. Yes, I want it."

CHAPTER 23

RUE

My head ached with a dull throb but I'd taken some pain relievers, so it should calm down soon. Still, I needed quiet, and the interview room was perfect for that. I curled up on the floor using a backpack as a pillow and relaxed.

Channeling had taken it out of me big time.

"You'll feel better soon," Jilyana said from the doorway. "Your body is healing. I can see it."

I sat up slowly, nursing my head. "See it?"

"Yes...your aura..." She crossed the room and lowered herself onto the floor beside me. "It's hard to explain, but there is energy around all living things, and it has various colors. The colors mean different things. Yours is wounded right now, but there are areas of regeneration, so you are healing. But your friend..." She caught her bottom lip between her teeth. "The human male you are close to...Bastian, is it?"

"I know. He's dying." It was the first time I'd said it out loud, admitted it, and a cold numbness spread through me. "We all know."

She nodded slowly. "I wish I could heal him, but his body isn't wounded in a way that can be healed. It's as if...as if the damage has been sewn into the fabric of his being, and even if it was fixed it would spawn once again." She frowned. "I can't understand how that can be."

"The sweeper serum caused it. The celestials gave it to us to allow us to wield celestial blades and kill the monsters. Apparently, it contains a little celestial light which...well, it's harmful to humans." My soul was woven with a fragment of Shemyaza's. If I'd been a sweeper, I'd have been safe from the harmful effects. Not that it mattered now. "It makes no sense because the celestials are somehow using human emotion to create celestial energy. How can something that *comes* from us be harmful to us?"

"Energy in one form can be safe, useful even, but if it's altered, it can be harmful, kill even. I'm sorry this has happened to you."

"Yes...me too."

"I wish that I could help." She fell into silence for a

while. "I want to do good," she said abruptly. Then she tucked in her chin with a sigh. "I need to do good to make up for...everything." When she looked up, her eyes glistened with unshed tears. "I loved him. I truly did."

"I think Michael loved you too, in his own way. He just...loved himself more."

She licked her lips nervously. "No, not Michael... Shem. I fell in love with him, and it was stronger than what I felt for Michael."

My heart sank, but I wasn't surprised. I'd sensed this. "You couldn't have loved him that much. You betrayed him, after all." My words came out sharper than intended.

She flinched. "I had no choice. If I'd backed out, then they would have killed me."

She had no idea how love worked. "Maybe it's different for humans, but when we love someone, truly love someone, we would give our lives to protect them in a heartbeat."

She exhaled heavily. "You're right. We are different. Maybe you are what he needs. I'm glad he's found happiness with you, and I hope that one day he can forgive me for what I did."

"I hope so too."

Bee popped her head into the room. "We're back."

WE HAD A BUS. An actual vehicle to get these people to safety. Yes, we'd have to go on foot part of the way, but this increased the odds of getting everyone to the church alive.

Bastian and Bee had also made a couple of stops on the way to grab some sleeping bags and camping gear from a local hiking equipment store. We already had a camping stove, but they'd picked up two more. Still, we all agreed it was too risky to cook food, as the smell could draw the predators at night.

We did heat water for tea and coffee though, and Mira handed out cookies from a box she'd packed. They'd been freshly made the day before and tasted delicious.

For a little while, the mood in the bank was optimistic. But then night fell and the distant, and sometimes not-so-distant, howls of monsters reminded everyone how close to danger we were.

Sissy kept the children occupied with stories and quiet games until it was time for them to go to sleep.

The hours ticked by, and silence fell as one by one our party drifted off into slumber, confident that the watchers would protect them at their most vulnerable.

These were my people. My responsibility. But the

watchers were my people too now. My family. And they needed sleep as well.

Shem sat by the main doors, his back to the wall, one knee up, elbow resting on it.

I crouched in front of him. "You and the watchers need to sleep. Bastian, Bee, and I can take turns to keep watch."

The corner of Shem's mouth lifted. "You're sweet, but no. I won't sleep knowing that you're not beside me."

He said it so casually that it took a moment for the deeper meaning of his words to hit, but when it did... ah...my heart.

I'd promised myself I wasn't going to do this yet but... "What you said in the mall when you thought Michael was going to take me..."

He slow-blinked and fixed his intense gaze on me. "I meant it."

For a moment I couldn't breathe.

"I needed you to know," he said. "Now you do."

And I needed him to know. "I love you too, Shem."

His nostrils flared, and his beautifully feral face softened. "Good, because one-sided affection is never fun."

I let out a soft laugh. "True." I made myself comfortable on the floor beside him and rested my head on his shoulder.

"What are you doing?" he asked.

I slung my arm around his waist. "I won't sleep knowing that you're not beside me."

His chest rumbled, and he put his arm around me to allow me to settle cozily against him. "Five minutes," he said, in his warm, gravelly voice. "Then I want you to get into the sleeping bag Bastian picked up for you."

"Mmmm." I closed my eyes. "Ten minutes."

His chest vibrated in a soft chuckle. "Ten minutes, then."

I woke much later, tucked into warmth with Bastian's large frame curled around me.

His breath warmed my neck, and his arm pinned me to his chest. My eyelids were heavy. But I forced myself to stay awake a moment to revel in this contact and in the comfort of Bee's soft snores and the collective warmth of the bodies in the room. We were surviving, and nothing was impossible if we stuck together.

I caught movement by the door followed by the gleam of orange eyes, then nothing.

My pulse spiked.

Why the fuck was Jilyana watching me sleep?

CHAPTER 24

Dawn came quickly, and everyone packed and gathered, ready to make the trip to the bike store and the bus that waited there.

"Are you certain you have the energy for this?" Shem asked Jilyana. "We can make room on the bus for the children if you can't transport them to the safe zone."

"I can do it." She smiled up at him warmly, and my stomach contracted. I didn't like the way she looked at him.

Shem stepped back with a slight frown. "Very well. Penemue, Amaros, you'll keep her and the children safe."

"You'll have to travel to this spot." Zaq held up a map for Jilyana to look at.

She studied it for several beats. "This doesn't help me. I need to visualize where I'm going."

"Really?" Bee asked. "Did you visualize the warehouse before you transported Rue and the watchers out of the mall?"

"No...and that could have gone very wrong, but we were on a time constraint. I acted on instinct, and we got lucky. I won't take that risk with these human children."

"So how will you visualize the church?" Penemue asked.

"By looking into the mind of someone who's been there." Her gaze went to Shem, and once again, my stomach tightened. "I'll need to place my fingers on your temple, and you'll need to allow me in."

Shem tensed, and it didn't take a genius to work out why. She'd been in his head before. Taken over his mind and his body and caused him to fracture the Morningstar, and now she was asking him to open his mind to her again? Could she be that clueless?

I wouldn't allow her to touch him. "I've been there. You can use me."

Her gaze flew to mine. "Oh...That can work too."

"Good." I gave her a tight-lipped smile. "After all, you've been in my head before."

She looked sheepish. "I'm sorry about that." She looked genuinely upset at having violated my privacy.

Was I being overly harsh? "It's fine. Let's do this so we can be on our way."

She slipped past Shem to stand in front of me. "Close your eyes, relax, and imagine yourself back at the church."

I forced my tense shoulder muscles to unwind and closed my eyes. I was back in the church, sitting on the wooden pew with the stained-glass windows around me. It was safe here. Quiet and warm.

My senses prickled, and then a presence joined me.

"This is nice," Jilyana said from the spot beside me. "Plenty of space for everyone."

"There are a few back rooms too. A kitchen and another floor."

"We can move the pews to make space in here. I need to see more. Take me through the building."

I walked across the main room and to the left, through a door that led to a short corridor and into the side room where Shem and I had—

My back was pressed to the wall and Shem was inside me.

"Yes, good girl, that's it. Take it," Shem said, his voice thick with arousal.

Fuck! I shook off the memory, and we were back on the pew. "Um...That wasn't—"

"It's fine," Jilyana said tightly. "We can go back now."

I opened my eyes to Jilyana's flushed face.

159

"I have what I need now," she said, ducking her head.

"Good. Gather the children," Shem said. "Let's do this."

Sammy was too weak to go anywhere without Clara, but Jilyana was confident she could carry one more person. It was strange watching them vanish before our eyes.

"Let's hope they made it okay," Sarq said.

"We'll find out tomorrow," Tumiel replied.

The bus had cut our journey in half. We'd be at the church by sunset tomorrow if all went well.

With the children gone, the adults were more than ready to get moving.

Shem split the watchers into pairs and assigned a small group of humans to each pair. It wasn't far to the bike store, but we'd experienced enough to know that anything could go wrong.

"Stay together," Shem said. "Stay close to your assigned watchers. Do as they say, and you might live."

I studied the faces around me, expressions ranging from fearful to determined, and vowed that I'd make sure all of them made it to safe zone twelve.

CHAPTER 25

We made it to the bike store and through to the garage without incident. The bus waited in the gloom like a silent savior, all fueled up and ready to go.

"Come on." Bee ushered everyone along. "Everyone inside."

The air pulsed with relief as people lined up to board the ride.

"Here, you'll need this." Zaq pressed his map into Bastian's hands. "I marked the route."

"Thank you," Bastian said.

"We'll travel by day and hide out during the night," Zaq said. "First location is marked on the map. It looks like a detour, but it only takes us a half hour off track. It's the only safe spot before the church."

"There are supplies there," Tumiel added.

It made sense to stop. We couldn't risk being attacked by razor beaks once the sun went down. The bus would be too much of a target, and last time...

My throat pinched as I recalled the last time we'd traveled in a bus. That night all those weeks ago when we'd fled our settlement, and my father...

No. We wouldn't make the same mistake twice.

I spotted Sissy, hanging back with a look of wariness. Was she recalling the last time we'd traveled by bus too?

I gave her a nod. "We're good. We won't be traveling at night."

She offered me a shaky smile. "Good to hear."

Shem gently gripped my nape, massaging the tense muscles as people finished boarding.

Once everyone was settled, Bastian took the driver's seat, and for a moment, it was Javier in the seat. He'd been our driver the last time, but he was gone now. Killed by Michael and his purge.

Bitterness stung my throat.

I'd trusted Michael.

How could I have been so blind?

"Go on," Shem said softly. "Get inside."

I climbed up and noted how packed the space was. No room for the watchers.

My panic must have shown on my face because Shem chuckled. "We don't travel in confined spaces, Rue. We'll ride on top or fly."

Of course they would.

I took the seat behind Bastian and placed my hand on his shoulder. "You remember how to drive?"

"It's like riding a bike, right?" His words were flippant, but his tone held nerves.

"That's what they say." I squeezed his shoulder.

But the muscles beneath my hand remained tense. He was afraid that he'd fail. But this was Bastian, and machines were his forte.

I leaned in so that my lips brushed the shell of his ear. "Hey, you've got this."

Tumiel shoved open the garage doors, and light flooded into the vehicle.

"Here goes everything." Bastian turned the key, and the engine purred to life.

People cheered, and my heart lifted, buoyed by the sound of hope.

We rolled onto the sunlit road, and a moment later soft thuds on the roof told me that several watchers had taken perch. The muffled flap of wings followed, and when I peered out of the window, Shem and Sarq were visible, flying low and parallel to the bus.

We were on our way.

WE REMAINED on the main road for a few hours. This road had once connected the major towns and cities of this world. It was cracked and dusty now, overgrown with weeds and tree roots so that we had to slow several times to navigate it. But it was the quickest and safest route during the day, at least if we hoped to avoid the monsters.

The celestials were another issue.

Daytime was when they'd be searching for us, but the watchers scouting the air would warn us if they spotted any incoming sentinels.

"An hour and we should see the slip road we need to take," Bastian said. "Can you check the map and make sure I have it right?"

I grabbed the map off the dash and sat back to study it. "Yeah, there'll be a signpost, or not. We need to keep an eye for the exit. "

"Got it."

I glanced down the bus where most of the people were fast asleep. The gentle rhythmic motion of the drive was soothing, and I'd had to stifle more than a couple of yawns myself.

But if we were tired, what did that say about Bastian? "Are you all right to keep driving?"

"Doesn't matter. I'm the only one that can."

That wasn't strictly true. "Bee and I can drive too."

"A bus?" He sounded impressed.

"Never driven a bus, but it can't be that different to

the rovers the settlement had dotted about for us to use."

"In that case, I might take you up on your offer if my concentration starts to flag."

A thud on the roof was followed by the scrape of talons on metal as the watchers switched places from coasting on the roof to flying.

A moment later, Shem's face appeared at my window. He grinned at me, upside down. I placed my palm on his cheek through the glass and made a kissy face.

"You two are adorable," Bee said from across the aisle.

Bastian chuckled. "I highly doubt Shem would appreciate being labeled adorable."

"Agreed," Bee said. "Doesn't change the facts."

Someone snort-snored loudly behind us, and Bee jumped. I bit back my laugh.

"Looks like everyone is relaxed," Bee said.

"You should get some sleep too."

"Nah." She leaned back in her seat. "I kinda feel like I've slept a little too much, you know?"

Was she referring to her time in the mixer?

"Do you think Michael made it?" she asked suddenly.

"I hope not."

"Me too, but...I think he did."

"The bond?"

"Yeah, I kinda feel like I'd know if he hadn't…"

"Yeah, I feel the same way about Gabriel. He's alive…I'm just not sure for how much longer."

"If he's as savvy as you said, then he'll make it," Bastian said. "At least long enough for us to finish our mission."

Our mission.

Yes, that's what this was.

The bus swerved, and Bastian righted it quickly. "Yeah, I think one of you might need to take the wheel."

"I'll do it!" Bee said eagerly.

Bastian decelerated so Bee could take the wheel and settle into the driver's seat, then claimed her vacated spot and beckoned me to join him across the aisle.

Snuggled beside him, it was impossible not to relax.

"Sleep," he said. "I'll watch over you."

I wanted to protest, but my eyes were already closing, the familiar lethargy of oblivion seeping through my limbs.

Sleep sounded good right—

"Watch out!" Bastian bellowed.

Bee screamed.

The bus swerved and then something slammed into us with enough force to send me and Bastian flying into the window.

CHAPTER 26

SHEM

We don't see the creature until it's too late. It appears as if out of nowhere—at least seven feet tall and five feet wide, on all fours. And that's the extent of my assessment before it slams into the bus with a sickening crunch that makes the side of the vehicle crumple inward.

The watchers on the roof are thrown off and join me in the air as the bus topples onto its side. The awful sound of metal scraping on cement assaults my ears as the bus slides several feet before coming to a halt.

My heart shoots into my throat, cutting off my warning cry, and the humans' screams rend the air as if to compensate.

The beast rears back, and jets of pale pink goop hit the underside of the bus.

It's something new.

Something we've not come across before.

Armor plates run down its back and over its head, which is shaped like the head of a hammer. Its bulbous eyes sit at either end, and in between is a mouth designed for tearing flesh.

"Attack!" Sarq bellows, jolting me out of my shock.

The watchers fly at the beast, but I aim for the bus, my instinct to get to Rue.

The beast vanishes before the watchers can touch it.

"What the fuck?" Sarq says. "Where did it go?"

I land on the side of the bus, and for a moment the world is still, the only sound the cries of shock and pain from within the metal contraption. But there's a strange smell in the air...sulphur and...Is that fuel?

Fuck! "Get them out. Get everyone out now. This thing is going to explode. We can worry about the beast later." I press my face to the windows that peer up at the sky and call out a warning. "Steer clear. I need to smash the glass." I wait a moment before punching out a window.

I barely register the scrape and sting of glass as I clear the aperture. With the bus on its side, everyone is crushed against each other close to the ground.

Frightened eye whites gleam up at me, but the eyes I want to see are absent. "Rue? Rue!"

"I'm here. Get them out." Her voice is muffled, and my heart squeezes painfully in my chest, and for a moment I care nothing for any of these people. All I want is to shove them aside and reach for her, wherever she may be. But I can't see her. She's hidden somewhere beneath all these insignificant bodies.

I have to clear them. "I'm coming. Don't move."

"I can't move," she admits.

"I have her," Bastian calls out. "Get the others off us."

He sounds breathless. They're hurt. I need to get to them now.

Tumiel lands on the window farther down and punches it out, calling out for Bee.

We work in a frenzy, hauling people out of the window while Zaq ushers them to the other side of the road, ordering them to stay together. Baraqel and his troop surround the humans, eyes on the road as they scan for threats.

The beast is gone, but it might come back. The priority is clearing this vehicle before it explodes.

Move, humans. Out of the way. I practically fling them to safety, searching the dark interior for the only humans I care about.

"I've got Rue," Tumiel calls out a moment later.

The knot in my belly unravels.

I look over at her cradled in Tumiel's arms for a moment, before he hands her to Sarq. There's blood on her face. She's hurt.

Fuck everyone else.

"Shem?" Bastian calls out from inside the bus.

I grab his arm and haul him out. My heart hammers against my ribs with the desire to go to Rue. I can't. Not yet. But Bastian can. "Go to Rue."

Bastian clambers off the bus and jogs across the road.

"That's it," Tumiel says. "We have everyone."

He leaps off the bus and grabs Bee's hand. They cross the road to the others. I spot Rue, and our gazes meet. She's safe with Bastian. Bloody but safe. She beckons for me to hurry.

A quick check confirms the bus is empty, and I join the others on the side of the road.

Rue melts into my arms. "What happened? What hit us?"

"We're not sure," Sarq answers for me because my throat is too tight to speak.

I smooth her hair back, lightly skimming her temple and forehead, looking for a wound.

"Ouch." She pulls away.

There's a cut on her forehead, but it's beginning to clot.

"Did you kill it?" Bastian asks.

"No, it vanished," Sarq says.

"What do you mean?"

"I mean just that. It vanished into thin air."

"How is that possible?" Rue asks.

"I don't know. But Penemue might, if he was here."

"Can we fix the bus?" someone asks. "If we can get it back on its wheels?"

"The fuel tank is damaged," Bastian says. "I started to feel dizzy from the fumes before I made it out. Kerosene might not explode but with a leaking tank, the bus is a lost cause."

Someone begins to cry, and another human hushes them.

"How far out are we?" Bee asks. "How long will it take on foot?"

Bastian pulls the map from his back pocket and hands it to Zaq, who takes a moment to study it.

"With the bus we would have made it to the first safe zone an hour before sunset, but now…"

"We'll be traveling on foot at night," Rue finishes for him. "In which case we need to get moving."

"All the supplies…" Mira sniffs. "Zaq…everything is gone."

He puts his arm around her. "We have supplies at the safe zones, and we can get more." He kisses her temple. "It'll be all right."

She wipes at her eyes and nods. "Yes. Safe zone. Everyone pull yourselves together. We've got a trek to make, and we're going to do it in double time. Okay?"

She receives a chorus of okays.

I may be the official leader of this group, but Mira is the glue that keeps the humans bound together. I can't do this without her.

She looks over at me and gives me a nod.

I clear my throat. "All right, we move out. Same formation as before, stick to your watchers, stay close and—"

A crack splits the air, and a chorus of roars follow.

Four large shapes surround the toppled bus.

Four of the armored monsters.

The pink goop on the bus glows brightly. It's a marker. A beacon. The thing vanished to fetch more of its kind, and now they're here, circling the vehicle.

They haven't seen us yet. We can slip into the woods behind us, into the shadows and—

One of the monsters rams the bus.

The humans by the side of the road scream, and the monsters freeze.

"Fuck," Sarq grits out as all four beasts turn their heads to zero in on us.

CHAPTER 27

RUE

The air was charged with danger. The road an arena of death and destruction. We couldn't stay on it any longer.

"Get off the road!" I ushered the nearest people down the incline that led to the ominous woodland beyond.

"Back up! Everyone back up now!" Bastian ordered.

I skidded to a halt by the incline, dropping low to make myself small.

The monsters were twice the size of a watcher, and their front legs also doubled as arms, allowing them to rear up to grab at their quarry.

My body itched to jump into the fray and help, but I'd be nothing but a hindrance, a distraction, cannon fodder in a fight that required the kind of raw power I didn't have.

It was strength, and claws, and talons.

Where was Shem?

There!

He grappled with a huge beast solo, his hands on the hammer-like protrusions of its head. The beast was strong, forcing Shem back across the ground in a slide that would have skinned the soles of his feet if he hadn't had thick leathery soles.

My pulse beat hard in my throat, blood rushing in my head. Come on, Shem. Come on...

In a sudden move, Shem let go of the beast's head, spinning away then back to shoulder-slam its torso and shove it across the cement. The monster lost its balance and hit the ground on its side like the bus. Shem attacked its soft underbelly, bellowing for an assist that brought two more watchers to his side.

The cloying scent of blood filled the air.

One down, three to go.

Baraqel and his team succeeded in toppling a second beast, and once again they tore out its insides, and now that they had a system, it was all claws on deck.

Zaq zoomed back and forth to confuse the beasts, providing the distraction that the others needed to pin them and take them down.

These fuckers were big, but they weren't smart, and

their bulk also meant that once they were on their side, it was difficult for them to get back to their feet.

"Yes!" Bastian grabbed my hand and squeezed. "They've got this. One more left."

Hope and triumph bloomed between us. Bastian shifted from side to side with nervous energy that would usually be expended on the battlefield. But today he was a bystander like me. Unable to assist in the fight.

But we weren't helpless or useless by any means.

I turned to check on my people huddled on the edge of the woods, and a strange shudder rippled over my skin.

I shook it off. "We should scout the woods while they finish off the monsters."

Bastian nodded. "Good call." We'd barely made it down the hill on the side of the road when the eerie squawk of razor beaks echoed in the air above us.

My stomach shot up into my chest as my gaze whipped up to the sky. The huge predatory birds appeared above us, coming seemingly out of thin air just like the armored creatures.

Dark mist clung to their vast prehistoric wings, entering our atmosphere in thick streams before spreading out to create a misty layer of gloom between us and the sun.

This couldn't be happening.

It was daytime.

It was fucking daytime.

A vise crushed my chest, leaving me panting in panic, because if the winged beasts were here during daylight hours, it could only mean one thing.

The rules had changed.

THE RAZOR BEAKS swooped in attack, three aimed at the watchers and two aimed at us humans clustered by the side of the road.

"RUN!" Bastian grabbed my hand, and we made a break for the woods.

We ducked into the tree line, making it impossible for the razor beaks to dive low enough to grab any of us. The flying monsters pulled up, their horrific clawed feet scraping the tops of the trees so it rained leaves for a moment.

"Oh gods, oh gods," someone sobbed.

"It's all right. We're all right if we stay under cover," Mira consoled.

"Stay together," Bee ordered. "We're safe here. It's daytime."

Our gazes locked, and I shook my head slightly, because was that even true anymore? "Stay quiet. Just...in case."

Someone whimpered and was harshly told to shut up by Mira.

"One armored beast and five razor beaks," Bastian said. "We're good. There are nine watchers out there. They can take them."

My stomach trembled. "I need to check—"

Bastian made a grab for me. "Stay. I'll go."

I shook him off. "No, I need to check because if they're flagging, then..." I gave him a pointed look, hoping that he wouldn't make me say it.

"Dammit, Rue..."

"I'll have to."

"I know."

The power thrummed inside me as I slipped out from cover, keeping low, eyes on the sky where six, no, seven razor beaks and eight airborne watchers flew. I spotted Sarq, Tumiel, Zaq, Baraqel, and his troop.

But Shem...Where was Shem?

A fist of panic formed in my belly. I had to check, had to see...

The hill, which had been easy to navigate when descending, felt like a mountain when climbing, but I scrambled to the top, unnoticed by the beasts above, who were too busy fighting off the watchers. The ground was bloody and strewn with the intestines of the armored beasts, but where was Shem?

There propped up against one of the dead beasts, hands on his belly as he held himself together...

No...No, no, no!

"Rue!" Bastian cried out from behind me.

But I was already on the road, running toward Shem.

He looked up, eyes flaring with shock at the sight of me. "No! Get back!"

Like hell. I skidded to a halt, falling to my knees beside him as a wave of déjà vu washed over me. For a moment, I was back in the shack surrounded by monsters with Jarrod propped against a pillar bleeding out while Pip, my medic, tried to patch him back together, then I was on the road, surrounded by my frightened people with a single razor beak attacking us and my father propped against a pile of dead bodies begging me to end his life.

"Go," Shem said. "You have to..." He coughed up blood.

I gripped his jaw and forced him to look into my eyes, which blazed with heat. "Let's get one thing straight, Shem. I'm never, *ever* leaving you, you understand me?"

I pressed my palm to his chest and opened the channel to the Morningstar power. It blazed bright, stealing my vision and flooding me with intense heat.

Someone screamed loud and shrill.

"Rue. Rue, let it go. Close it. You need to close it."

But the door was wide open, the power flooding

out, eager to be free. I couldn't do it. I couldn't shut it. It was too heavy. It wouldn't budge.

I got you. Shem's presence bloomed inside my mind, his chest pressed to my back, his hands over mine as I shoved at the door.

Together we slammed it shut.

I slumped in his arms, inhaling the sharp iron scent of his blood.

The death cries of the razor beaks filled the air as Shem held me to his chest, his heart beating hard and fast.

"Oh fuck, thank fuck." Bastian stroked my hair.

I slowly lifted my head, my gaze grazing Shem's jaw, then rising to meet his eyes, where a tumult of emotions danced.

"You're insane," he said gruffly.

"No," Bastian replied for me. "She's a scout, and we never leave a man behind."

I looked up at him and smiled. "I love you." Then to Shem, "I love you both so fucking much."

Behind us, the razor beaks fell to the earth one by one. The ground trembled with the impact, and Shem and Bastian held me tighter.

The watchers remained in the sky for a moment, their forms silhouetted by a rapidly setting sun, but there was something different about them that I couldn't define. As they came in to land and the sun was no longer sat at their backs, the difference became apparent. Horns and tusks were gone, and their skin was more a rose color rather than orange or red.

Every single one of them had evolved a little.

I'd done this, and although tired, I wasn't hurt by it.

I'd done this, and I wasn't unconscious.

Yes, something had changed.

But what?

CHAPTER 28

SHEM

The sun is setting, and the woods are getting darker. We move silent and fast, humans flanked by watchers like sheep being herded.

There are so few of them left, and we can't afford to lose any more.

I won't fail them.

Our next hideout is a couple of hours away on foot, but if we keep up this pace, we might make it there sooner. Now that we're not in the bus, we can take shortcuts.

Zaq leads the way, scouting ahead to check for danger, but I'm no longer sure it matters, because I'm no longer certain that danger won't simply materialize in front of us out of thin air.

We're all thinking it, but there's no time to discuss it. We've got to stay quiet and keep moving.

Rue walks between Bastian and me. He's obviously just as loath to be away from her as I am. Another pair of eyes on her is good.

My gaze drops to her for a beat, noting the dark smudges beneath her eyes, the only indication of the toll channeling took on her. She healed me in a matter of moments and fed all the watchers Morningstar power in the process, yet she's on her feet. Walking on her own steam. She should be more hurt, more damaged, because the expulsion of power...Well, I'm surprised the sentinels haven't found us by tracking it.

But it's more than that. More than Rue's stoic reaction to opening the channel. There's something in the air that's different. The sky is coated in a fine dark mist that came through with the razor beaks, and the distinct stench of sulphur lingers in the air even now.

"What was that?" Rue whispers. "Shem, what the fuck just happened? Those things came out of thin air."

"I'm not sure. We should wait to discuss this. Your people are already frightened."

"Good point."

"Do you think the sentinels will have sensed the power?" Bastian asks.

"The channel was open for mere moments." Which

could be enough, based on the amount of power, but they hadn't found us yet so... "We'll be fine."

Zaq whizzes back. "Woods ending. Field up ahead."

"Great, open ground," Rue mutters in an uncharacteristically cranky tone.

I can hardly blame her for being upset. Our plans, our safe haven, our home, have all gone to shit in the past few hours.

The watchers close in, tightening their net on the humans as we exit the woods onto a moonlit field. The sky is filled with stars tonight, but they seem muted as if a veil hangs between us and them.

"There's something in the air," Bastian says. "What is it?"

"I don't know."

Rue slows her pace and presses her fist to her chest.

"What's wrong?" Bastian and I ask at the same time.

"I feel weird," she says. "My chest feels hollow and warm."

"The Morningstar power?"

"No, this is...It's something else." She exhales. "And it's gone."

My concern is echoed on Bastian's face.

Could channeling have done a deeper damage? One we can't see? I need to get Rue to safety fast so we can check her over. If anything happens to her...I can't lose her. Not for the world.

RUE

The strange hollow feeling inside my chest was a consistent flutter now and not wholly unpleasant. It was the kind of feeling I associated with nerves of excitement or anxiety, but I was far from excited, and anxiety was too tame a word to describe how I felt about our situation right now. Hypervigilant was more apt, but this sensation inside me...it didn't quite fit.

Shem had his gaze fixed on the terrain. He was in watcher mode, attention split between the sky, the road ahead, and the fields on either side of us.

We were less than an hour away from the safe zone where we'd spend the night before heading to the church tomorrow morning and an eerie silence had settled over the world, raising goosebumps on my skin and making the hairs on my nape quiver with foreboding.

Back when I'd been a scout and we'd been in dire situations, I'd focus on what I'd do once the shitty situation was over and we were back at base. I'd focus on something good and solid, like being in Jamie's arms or hanging out with Bee. I'd focus on a treat that I'd give myself, and right now, the image of being snuggled between Shem and Bastian was my reward. My treat for surviving.

I'd be safe, and warm, and I'd sleep...I'd fucking sleep so deeply with them both watching over me and—

An image of Gabriel filled my head, sudden and unexpected, followed by the poignant memory of the pressure of his lips on mine when he'd bonded with me in the Golden City. The memory dissipated just as quickly as it had flooded my mind. What the heck? But now I couldn't stop thinking about the auburn-haired celestial.

Where was he now? What had they done to him?

He was alive...He had to be. We were bonded, so surely I'd know if he was dead. I'd feel it, right? Something...

"Rue, are you all right?" Bastian asked.

"I'm fine." I fixed a smile on my face. "Just tired now."

"I can carry you."

"I'm fine. I'm not physically tired."

"Yeah, I get it."

Tension rippled through my body—a primal warning a moment before Zaq cried out in alarm.

"Incoming!"

"Fucking hell!" Bastian cried.

I spotted the ripper a moment later.

Larger than the ones we'd dealt with in Sector 4.

These were type 5, and they were headed down the road right at us.

"I didn't see them!" Zaq cried. "They weren't there a moment ago."

There was no time to debate. "Off the road! Move!" I led the humans off the road and into the field, not that it would do much good. The rippers could see us and smell us. There was no cover.

We were fucked.

They swarmed toward us. Too many for the watchers to engage. Too many to keep them off us.

"Run!" Bastian ordered. "Fucking run for the woods!"

The close-knit trees would make it harder for the rippers to get to us, they would slow them down. But slow didn't mean stop. Nothing could stop them.

We ran, boots beating the earth with the thunder of a multitude of talon-tipped legs behind us.

Bee ran alongside me, arms pumping hard, head pushed forward, and for a moment I was back on the road in Sector 4, running from the rippers with Bee at my side.

Behind us, the screech and scream of the creatures being attacked by the watchers tore at the silence that had shrouded us up until now.

Looking back wasn't an option.

The tree line rushed to meet us, but the air fizzed and two huge crabines erupted into our path out of nowhere.

They reared up, pincers clacking eagerly.

People screamed, skidding to a halt before veering left to get away from the creatures.

The crabines and the rippers clashed.

But there were more rippers then crabines.

They'd win, and then they'd come for us.

"Move!" We had to get into the forest while the fuckers were distracted.

The air crackled, and the tree line was blocked off by more crabines. "Get back!"

We were trapped, surrounded by the creatures with no watchers to protect us.

"What do we do?" Mira cried. "What do we do?"

My heart sank, and icy terror filled my veins. There was nothing.

This was the end.

Bee took my free hand as we faced the beasts, aware that more were at our back.

"Rue!" Shem cried from the distance, flying toward me. The watchers fought rippers on the road behind him, their forms dark silhouettes against a moonlit sky. "Rue, I'm coming!"

But he wouldn't make it in time, and even if he did, I couldn't, wouldn't leave my friends to save my skin, and the look on his face—dark and filled with a mixture of horror and regret—told me he knew it.

"It's okay." Bastian wrapped his arms around both Bee and me. "It's okay."

Everyone had stopped screaming, huddling together as the threat closed in.

Moments. And it would be over.

Lightning lashed down and incinerated a ripper, another blast hitting a crabine.

No. Not lightning, but celestial rays of power. Sentinels?

"Rue! It's Gabriel!" Bee cried.

I spotted Gabriel high above us, surrounded by armored reapers, their helms gleaming in the flashes of celestial light that jettisoned out of their scythes and smashed into the monsters, turning them to ash.

Gabriel scanned the ground, and his gaze finally fell on me. The flutter in my chest became a steady vibration, and a sob broke from my throat because it was him...of course that flutter had been him.

He'd come for me.

He'd found me.

The world dimmed, the screams and growls of the monsters died, and the reapers landed around us, huge monolithic beings exuding power that made the hairs on my body tremble with awareness. But my attention was focused on Gabriel, the cocky celestial with the stunning emerald eyes that were fixed intensely on me.

"Sorry I'm late," he drawled. "I got held up for a while. But prison cells are not my thing."

Maybe it was the whole near-death experience, but a wave of emotion washed over me, and before I could check myself, I'd bridged the distance between us and thrown my arms around his neck.

He hugged me back. "Ah, so you did miss me."

I choked back a laugh. "Yeah…yeah, I guess I did."

Erelim approached, dark hair mussed, helm tucked under his arm.

He dropped me a nod, and I mouthed *thank you*.

"We need to move. Now," Shem barked. "You can have your reunion later." His tone was cold, and a finger of ice slid up my spine.

I released Gabriel, swallowing the lump in my throat. He smiled thinly before taking in the two males who stepped forward to flank me.

"We're headed to the old farmhouse twenty minutes down the road," Shem said. "We've cleaned out the barn and set up traps to prevent access."

"We'll provide aerial support," Erelim said.

"Be careful," Bastian said quickly. "There's something odd going on. The monsters are appearing out of thin air."

Erelim nodded. "I know. I'll explain everything once we get to safety."

Shem turned to me. "You'll fly with me the rest of the way."

I wanted to argue, but I'd learned to read him, and although his tone was cold and commanding, his eyes held panic.

I stepped close and tipped my chin up to meet his gaze. "I'd love to."

Finding out what had happened to Gabriel would have to wait a little longer.

CHAPTER 29

SHEM

With the reapers and Gabriel to assist, we make it to the farmhouse without any further incident. I'm reluctant to let Rue out of my sight, but the people need her direction. Mira needs the support. So I release her with a kiss and the promise to find her once the area has been secured.

I've almost lost her twice in one day, and there's a ball of dread forming in my stomach. I can't afford to hone my focus in on her. I have a duty to protect humanity, to fix what I've broken, and yet...when it comes down to a choice, I'm afraid it will be Rue I choose, and damn the world.

Now Gabriel is here, another contender for her attention. Another male who wants what's mine. I don't like it, but I may not have a choice in the matter.

The way he looked at her...the way she ran to him... Boundaries must be set.

I find him on the roof of the main building, sitting with his back to the chimney, head tipped to the night sky. Was he watching me with Rue? Does he know how much his presence bothers me?

I don't know him well enough to read him. We always ran in different circles, but what I do know pegs him as a master strategist and manipulator, and before we fell, if I'd been asked to pick either Michael or Gabriel to put my trust in, I would have picked Michael.

There's something dark and distant about Gabriel. Something that's closed off and hidden.

"Come join me," he says. "It's a beautiful night."

"We need to talk."

"Spoilsport." He sighs and looks at me. "I assume Rue has told you what transpired during her stay in the Golden City?"

"Yes. She told me you bonded with her." I don't bother to keep the bitterness from my tone.

"Just the bonding part? She didn't tell you about our *intimate* chats in the bedchamber with a roaring fire for company and—"

My chest rumbles loudly in warning, cutting off his

words.

He arches a brow. "Use your words, Shem."

He wants words? I'll give him words. "Rue is *mine,* and your bond means nothing out here."

"It means nothing because I allow it to mean nothing." His tone is light, but his emerald gaze is cold. "But make no mistake, I will press the bond if it means saving her life. I will press the bond if it means protecting her from herself."

"And what the fuck does that mean?"

He stands slowly. "It means I won't allow her to be used as a pawn."

He thinks I'm using her? My confusion must show on my face because his stance relaxes a little.

He tips his head to the side, studying me for several beats. "Are you in love with her?"

The blunt question throws me for a moment, but the truth springs easily to my lips. "Yes. Yes, I am."

He balks in surprise as if he didn't expect me to admit it, and this gives me a little buzz of satisfaction. "I'm in love with her. She's mine. And that's all you need to know." My words come out as a warning growl.

He drops his gaze for a moment, shoulders rising and falling on a sigh. "I allowed the bond because it was my only way to protect her. It allowed me to find her tonight and save you."

"We were doing fine."

He looks up and rolls his eyes. "I thought we were

opening up here. Being honest. Play the damn game, Shem."

Fuck. What am I doing? Allowing my emotions to cloud this interaction with an ally. "We were doing fine until...until we weren't. You arrived just in time. You saved Rue, and I am more grateful than you could know." Fuck, it hurt to say it. But it was true. She'd be dead without his intervention. Twice now he'd saved her.

"Thank you for the acknowledgement," he says. "And, in the spirit of being honest, you should know that I've developed an attraction to Rue." A low growl vibrates in my chest, and he holds up his hand. "One that I will resist, even though I'm certain it's reciprocated."

I can't argue because I believe it's reciprocated too, and based on what he's said to me so far, there's something I need to know. "Will you use the bond to take her?"

Is that disgust on his face?

"I don't take what's not freely given," he says.

My words thrown back at me, but he couldn't have known that. There's no guile or deception in his tone.

He wants Rue, but he's willing *not* to act on his wants. "Why? Why not take what you want? You could do it without using the bond." I hate to say it, but my gut tells me it's true. "You could romance her."

He lets out a breathless laugh. "Romance...We have

bigger issues to deal with like fixing this world. Romance can wait." He arches a brow my way, as if to intimate that I should have been more careful not to fall into the romance trap.

"You have no idea how hard it is to resist Rue."

The corner of his mouth lifts. "Is that a challenge?"

"No. It's simply a fact."

He looks me in the eyes, locking gazes with me. "I'm not here to win Rue's affections. I'm here to help keep both you and her safe. Erelim, his reapers, and I are at your disposal. We won't rest until the relic is restored and the balance between the heavens and earth is put to rights, but you should know that the Dominion are planning something big. Michael's betrayal and my incarceration are all a part of it."

Back to business. I like this celestial. "Once we get to the church, we can have a meeting and swap information."

"And this church...How do you know it will be safe?"

"Trust me. Once we're there, you'll see for your-self...or maybe you won't." The celestials had bypassed the building as if they didn't see it, so will Gabriel be able to see it? I am interested to know.

"I love a good enigma," Gabriel says. "In the mean-time, why don't you and your watchers get some rest. The reapers and I can patrol. It's been a while since we looked upon a free sky."

I won't argue. My men could benefit from a reprieve, and these reapers have weapons that can incinerate the monsters. "How long before you run out of celestial power?"

"Don't worry, we have that under control."

"How?"

"Serum."

"Serum?"

"Yes, we have a bag of vials to keep us operational for several months. It's not a huge boost, but enough to stave off devolution so that we can help you."

It will have to do for now. "You and the reapers can take first watch. We'll take second."

"Works for us." Gabriel gives me a jaunty salute and launches himself off the roof and into the air, where Erelim hovers above the front lawn.

Having Gabriel and the reapers on our team will be a huge advantage, and yet, despite his assertion to the contrary, I can't help but feel that his presence might cause a rift between Rue and me. Sharing her with Bastian is easy because he's human, because like all humans, he will die. Bastian is temporary, but Gabriel...There will be no ridding myself of him.

There is only one way forward.

One way to prevent an inevitable rift between Rue and me.

Acceptance.

CHAPTER 30

RUE

There was a huge hole in the barn roof, and the inside was wet. It was evident that there'd been a storm recently that had destroyed it, but with the watchers and reapers on hand, it didn't take long to scope out the main house and get everyone situated.

There were a few battered sofas, four beds, and plenty of musty moth-eaten bedding to choose from.

Most of the windows were boarded up, and Bastian and Tumiel found some wood in the barn to board up the windows that weren't.

While Sarq arranged patrols, Bee and I did a walk-through of the place to look for any essentials that we could take with us to the church.

"Are you all right?" Bee asked me as I studied the contents of an upstairs wardrobe.

"I'm fine, why?"

"Gabriel is here."

My chest grew tight for some reason. "Your tone suggests that his being here should be a problem."

"Come on, Rue, you saw how Shem reacted when you hugged Gabriel. He got all growly and possessive."

"He sounded more cold and distant to me."

She gave me a flat look.

"Shem is fine. He knows that there's nothing going on between me and Gabriel. He knows the bond was made to protect me." Okay, so when Shem had brought it up over a week ago on our journey back to the mall, I'd needled him by saying I could fuck whoever I wanted to. It had ended up in his staking his claim in the most primal way, but I'd been pissed off. Wanting to make a point. The truth was simple. "I don't have romantic feelings for Gabriel."

"But you're attracted to him."

"It's irrelevant. It's the bond. But Gabriel and I can handle it, and Shem...Shem will be fine." I pulled out a couple of sweaters. "These are in good condition."

Bee rolled her eyes. "Fine, topic closed. Hand those to me. Oooh, boots."

We spent another twenty minutes upstairs and gathered a few more items of winter clothing before heading down the carpeted steps to the main floor.

The kitchen and dining room were to the left of the steps and the living room to the right. Voices drifted out from the kitchen, giving me pause.

"Why can't we stay here?" someone asked.

"Because it isn't safe," Mira replied. "The monsters could attack at any time. The longer we stay, the more chance of that happening."

"But we have the watchers to protect us," another voice piped up.

"It only takes one monster finding us then getting away to summon more, and even the watchers will be overwhelmed. You saw what happened out there."

Mira had it under control, it seemed.

Bee and I wandered into the lounge, which was nice and warm due to all the bodies crammed into it.

"Get the mattresses from upstairs and make beds there." Zaq pointed across the room. "You fetch the bedding."

People scurried about, following his orders.

The sofas had been moved around too. They were creating a safe sleeping space away from the windows.

A couple of watchers had positioned themselves by the large, boarded-up bay windows at the front of the house.

My skin tingled in that way that told me I was being watched. I turned to the arch leading to the hallway to find Shem watching me. He lifted his chin and jerked his head to the side, beckoning me.

I tapped Bee on the shoulder. "I'll be back."

She glanced at Shem. "Good luck."

I followed Shem through the back of the house into a small study. He closed the door and turned to face me.

"I've spoken to Gabriel."

For some reason, annoyance bit at me. "And?"

"I understand that you have a bond with him, unbreakable until death, and as much as I'd like to end him, I doubt it would do us any favors. So if you decide to share your body with him, then I won't stand in your way."

His gaze was flat. His jaw tense.

This was hurting him, and the strange tightness inside my chest grew. "I'm not romantically interested in Gabriel."

"Rue, your reaction to his arrival spoke volumes."

"I was relieved. Happy to see him, that's all." His smile was wry as if he knew a secret I didn't. "Dammit, Shem, I know my emotions, and they're not tangled up in Gabriel. He's an ally and a friend and that's all."

Shem looked like he wanted to say something, but long seconds passed before he spoke. "Your body is yours to give, Rue. As much as I would like to argue otherwise."

Was he serious? "Firstly, did you not hear what I just said, and secondly, what the fuck? What happened to all the *grrr* and *argh* and *you're mine* stuff?"

His eyes flashed with amusement. "I don't need to demand or stake my claim." He bridged the distance between us and gently gripped my throat so that my pulse beat wildly against his fingers. "This response... this breathless, wanton need that's coursing through you is all that I need to know who you crave."

My mouth was suddenly dry. I licked my lips to moisten them, pulse jumping harder when his gaze dropped to my mouth for a beat before flicking back up to my eyes. "You've got to stop doing this. It's not the time or place to get—"

He cut off my words with a crushing kiss, and I lost the thread of my thoughts, focused solely on the rasp of his tongue against mine and the burgeoning connection between us.

He broke the kiss, leaving me lightheaded. "No, Rue, I don't need to stake my claim. This..."—he cupped my pussy through my pants—"this ache is for me."

I pressed myself to his palm, biting back a whimper.

He kissed me again, tenderly this time, his hand slipping from my groin to slide around to the small of my back so he could press me to him.

My eyes heated, and I cupped his jaw, deepening the kiss as if I could somehow meld with him through this contact, to hold him to me and never be apart.

"I love you." He breathed the words against my lips. "That's enough."

This was a side of him I didn't know how to deal with—this softness that demonstrated compromise and understanding. It was new and made me love him even more.

"I have all I need, Shem. You and Bastian are all I need."

But the look in his eyes told me that he didn't believe that.

It was up to me to prove it.

CHAPTER 31

The house was quiet. People were settled and snug in their makeshift beds. A meal, warmth, and a roof over our heads were enough to banish the fear from the past few hours.

It seemed as if we were acclimatizing to our near-death lifestyle.

Adrenaline was our friend and vigilance a constant state of being which was a heavy ache in my bones and a constant pit in my stomach. The only carefree moments were those few seconds after waking when my mind was unburdened by the truth of our existence. Those precious moments were quickly dampened by the familiar weight of responsibility once my conscious mind stepped into gear.

We were safe for now, so I sat at the dining room

table sipping bitter tea and enjoying the heck out of it, because it was warm and felt good as it hit my belly.

Small pleasures mattered.

This slice of normality mattered.

Bee had retired for the evening, curled up beside Tumiel. I'd sleep when Bastian and Shem returned from a final sweep of the grounds. Curling up alone, even with blankets and pillows to hand, didn't appeal. But my guys would be back soon.

The reapers were doing first shift on patrol, and Shem and the watchers had taken on doing a full sweep of the grounds to look for any potential threats, like herald's claw nests and the likes.

But there was another reason keeping me up. The niggly feeling that I was neglecting to consider something. That I was forgetting something important. The thought flirted with my mind, hovering on the fringes of my consciousness before giving me the finger and vanishing altogether.

I massaged my temples, staunching my annoyance. It'd come to me once I stopped trying to latch on to it.

"Any more of that left?" Gabriel said from the doorway.

He looked weatherworn—his hair tousled and falling across his forehead in a way that made him seem young and carefree. But the ancient weariness in his emerald eyes put paid to that illusion. Those eyes had seen death and destruction, trauma and pain. And for a moment, I could see it too. Feel it.

My breath caught as a crushing weight settled on my chest.

Gabriel blinked sharply, and the vise-like grip on my lungs eased as the strange connection that had established itself between us cut off.

"Is that tea?" he asked.

I cleared my throat. "Yes."

"Could I have some?"

"I didn't know celestials drank tea."

"We don't. Not usually, but I'll make an exception today." He grabbed a cup from the sideboard where several freshly rinsed ones sat, then poured himself an inch of tea.

I bit back a smile because it was obvious that he didn't want any. He was trying to form a connection with me. He didn't need to. We were already bonded.

He took the chair next to mine and sat with his forearms resting on the table, hands cupping the mug. "It's strange being outside the city walls."

"How long has it been since you left?"

"Twenty years."

"But that...that's all the time you've been here on earth."

"Yes. There was no need for me to leave."

In other words, he hadn't been allowed to leave. "I'm glad you escaped."

205

"Me too." He sipped the tea and made an *ick* face.

I reached out and touched his arm. "You don't have to drink it."

"Just as well, it's foul." He set the cup down. "I spoke with Shem."

"Yes, he told me."

He turned his chair to face me, then took my hands in his. His fingers were warm, his firm grip sending a pleasant tingle through me. "Our bond doesn't need to mean anything. You don't *owe* it anything." His gaze was soft with sincerity. "Emotions were heightened in the Golden City. Between us..."

He was referring to the intense moments of attraction between us. Saying they didn't matter. Good. I mean, that was good, and the hollow pit in my belly didn't mean anything. I was probably just hungry.

And, he was waiting for me to reply. "I know. I understand why you did it. I'm grateful. I'm grateful that you're here with us. I never should have trusted Michael."

His fingers flexed around mine. "I trusted him too, and I believe...I believe he truly meant to help us. But something changed."

"Yeah, he got a better offer. He wants power." I filled him in on what Michael had said to me in the tunnels back at the mall. "He wants to be in charge."

"He's a fool, and it's obvious he has no clue what the Dominion are planning."

"And you do? What are they planning?"

"I'm not sure, but we have pieces of information. Once we get to this safe zone of yours, we can put them together. One of the Powers that helped us escape gave me this." He held up a small silver object. "It contains information on the Dominion's plans. But we'll need a computer to access it."

"And where will we get one of those?"

His smile was tight. "There is a place we can go, but I'll share that information with you all once your humans are safe in the church."

"I'm glad you found us."

He smiled, and my heart beat a little faster. There was no denying his beauty. No escaping that I found it appealing.

"So am I." His gaze heated. "Did you think I was dead? Did you worry?"

"I worried, yes, but I knew you were alive. I'm not sure how...I just...did."

His attention dropped to my mouth, and my pulse fluttered in my throat. He released my hands and sat back in his seat with a neutral smile.

"The bond can be useful for such things. It's how I was able to track you."

That had been the plan all along: for him to find the relic we'd thought we were leaving behind, then join us outside the city walls by tracking me and...Oh...

The strange niggly thought that had been working

its way to the surface suddenly broke free. If Gabriel could track me using the bond, then it stood to reason that Michael could track Bee just the same.

How had we not thought of that?

"What is it?" Gabriel asked. "You've gone pale."

"Michael and Bee are bonded too."

His frown cleared. "Shit."

"What do we do? He could find us at any moment."

"There is only one thing we can do," he said, his expression solemn.

"What?"

"We have to sever their bond."

But there was only one way to sever the bond. "No!"

"Yes. Rue, we have to kill Bee."

CHAPTER 32

Waking up my best friend to tell her that I needed her to die hadn't been on my to-do list for the day.

To be fair, she took it better than I would have, at least once I explained the situation. But then, Bee was more pragmatic than me. She was the level head that made sure I didn't lose my shit. Even back at base, back on scout duty, she'd been my anchor.

So now, when I explained what needed to happen, she took it in stride, even though the rapid pulse fluttering at the base of her throat told me she was freaking out.

I was, too, and it wasn't me who had to have my soul yanked out of my body by a reaper, hoping he could successfully put it back.

Tumiel, Bee, Gabriel, Erelim, and I gathered in the kitchen with the door closed to discuss our simple but terrifying plan.

"The bond isn't just physical," Gabriel explained. "But the death of the body that houses it will end it."

"I'll extract your soul, which will cause death to your body," Erelim explained. "But if I can put it back quickly, then you should live once more."

"You've never done this before, have you?" Bee asked.

"No," Erelim said. "But the theory is sound."

"This is too dangerous," Tumiel said. "What if it goes wrong? What if you can't put her soul back?"

"There is that risk," Erelim said. "I can't discount it as a possibility."

"But in *theory* it can be done." I looked from Gabriel to Erelim. "We have to try."

It had to work, because it was our only hope, otherwise Bee would have to leave or risk exposing us all.

"I want to do this," Bee said. "I'd rather die here than get eaten by some fucking monster out there on the road alone."

"You won't be alone," Tumiel said. "If you leave, I'll leave with you."

Bee looked up at him, stunned. I could only imagine the tumult of emotions she was feeling. I'd seen how close the two of them had become, but his words now confirmed it.

"All the more reason to stay and do this," Bee said finally. "Out there, Michael will find me, and if he finds me, he'll find you too." Her throat bobbed. "He'll kill you."

Tumiel's jaw ticked. "I'm not afraid of death."

"Yeah, me neither. But I won't be responsible for the death of others." She looked to Erelim. "Do it."

Tumiel looked like he had more to say, but he pressed his lips together. Arguing further was pointless, and he knew it.

"We should do it in the barn," Bee said. "If it goes wrong, you can leave my body there."

I gripped her hand and squeezed. "It won't go wrong." I had faith in Erelim.

She looked me in the eye, her expression grave. "If it *does* go wrong, then it's nobody's fault, understand. I'm grateful to have come this far. To have made it out of that fucking crazy city and had time with you and..." She looked at Tumiel. "I'm just grateful."

Tumiel exhaled through his nose and reached out to gently caress her cheek. "So am I."

She leaned into his touch for a moment before straightening and taking a breath. "Let's do this. Michael could be tracking me right now for all we know."

"Have you felt strange in your chest? Like a fluttering sensation?"

She swallowed hard and nodded. "Yeah. On the

road. But not for a little while now. Is that him tracking me?"

Fuck. "I think so."

"Then we need to act fast." She headed for the door. "Come on."

I followed her out of the house and into the night with a block of ice forming inside me because this felt like an execution, and all we could do was hope for rebirth.

"WHAT'S GOING ON?" Shem joined us in the barn as Bee lay down on a pile of dry hay Tumiel had managed to find. "What are you doing?" He closed the door. "Rue?"

"Erelim is going to extract Bee's soul from her body," Gabriel replied for me. "She's bonded to Michael, and he could use that bond to track her. Death can sever the bond."

"But it's risky," Tumiel added quickly. "Extracted souls aren't usually put back into their bodies."

Shem's eyes narrowed speculatively. "But it can be done." His gaze flicked to me, and it wasn't difficult to read his thoughts.

If this worked on Bee, then it might work on me and my bond to Gabriel.

"Don't think it," Gabriel said smoothly to Shem. "My bond with Rue is essential to our operation. Having me connected to her gives us an advantage."

Shem smiled thinly. "I'm no fool, Gabriel. I'm aware of how to utilize my resources."

"So I'm a resource now?" I kept my tone light to disguise the fact that his words kinda hurt.

His gaze flew to meet mine. "Not you. Him." He jerked his thumb in Gabriel's direction. "He's the resource."

"Hey, can we get on with this?" Bee said. "My ass is getting cold. The hay's not that dry."

I knelt beside her and took her hand. "You come back to me, okay? You fight to come back."

She smiled up at me. "You know me. I don't go down without a fight. Besides, someone's got to keep you out of trouble."

But she'd been willing to sacrifice herself to save me all those weeks ago when we'd been chased by rippers. She'd been willing to offer her body as a diversion to allow me to get to safety, and now...now she was putting her life on the line to save everyone here.

"I love you, Bee. You can do this." I looked up at Erelim. "Losing her is not an option."

The others closed in around us, and Erelim asked, "Are you ready?"

"Yes. Let's get this over with," Bee said.

Erelim held up his scythe, and the air hummed with the weapon's power.

Bee sucked in a sharp breath and closed her eyes. "Fuck."

I squeezed her hand as the scythe arched down and stopped with the blade's tip lightly touching her chest. Her body tensed, and her eyes flew wide. She exhaled then...then nothing.

"Bee?" She lay still and silent and unbreathing. "Erelim?"

"I have her." He stood stiffly, teeth clenched. "One moment. I must...I must attune with the scythe and ask it to release the soul back into its old shell."

"It's not an old shell. It's her regular one."

"Yes, but the scythe sees it as redundant now. One moment."

His chest heaved, silver eyes swirling with flecks of gold as he slowly, deliberately forced the scythe back toward Bee's body.

The blade gleamed silver, and warmth radiated from it.

Bee...The energy was Bee. "Hurry."

But instead of tipping downward, the blade jerked upward and away from Bee's body.

"Argh!" Erelim's eyes flashed as he fought his weapon.

I'd seen him transfer a soul from a body to a

container in the Golden City, but for some reason, the scythe refused to let him put Bee's soul back into her flesh and bone body.

"It wants to keep it," Erelim said. "It's hungry. I can't...I can't fight it."

But Bee was there. In the blade. I could feel her essence. Her confusion and fear. She wanted back into her body. "Put her back. Put her back now!"

Gabriel stepped forward to help.

"Don't!" Erelim ordered. "Only a reaper can touch a scythe."

Heat flooded my limbs, and my head felt light and dizzy. Bee was dying. She was dying for real.

I had to help her. I had to help her back into her body.

I acted on instinct, pushing up on my knees to grab the staff of the scythe. Power slammed into me along with Bee's energy, and for a moment, my friend and I were one. I felt her love, her resilience, and her goodness as it flowed through me, down my arm and into her body through our joined hands.

Erelim tore the staff free of me a moment later.

Bee sat up with a gasp. "Fuck! Fuck, fuck, fuck." She stared at me wide-eyed. "I was in your head."

A crazy, breathless laugh escaped my lips, and I threw my arms around her neck, hugging her tight.

"How did you do that?" Erelim asked me.

My body tingled, hairs quivering with residual power. "I don't know. I don't know, and I don't care."

"She's a channel," Gabriel said. "I believe she acted on instinct, and on this occasion, it worked, but you cannot take such risks in the future." His tone had a bite that killed the warm fuzzy feeling in my chest.

I stared at him in disbelief. "I was saving my best friend."

"Your best friend is not more important than this world," Gabriel snapped.

"He's right," Shem said. "We need you alive, Rue."

They stood side by side, both glaring at me reproachfully.

I glared right back. "What's the point of a world where everyone you love is gone, *hmmm*?"

The anger in Gabriel's eyes dimmed, and Shem shook his head and walked away, clearly exasperated. Yes, they had a valid point. I knew how important I was, but I wouldn't apologize for saving Bee.

"They're right, Rue," Bee said softly. "You can't put your life at risk. Not even for me. But thank you. Truly."

"What's done is done," Shem said. "Everyone get some rest. We move at dawn."

I helped Bee to her feet. "How do you feel? Is the connection with Michael gone?"

"I feel a little woozy, but yeah, that weird feeling in my chest is gone. The connection is—"

The door to the barn flew open, and Zaq stood panting in the frame while the dark silhouette of watchers ran back and forth across the moonlit yard behind him.

"They're coming," he said. "The celestials are coming."

CHAPTER 33

Silence reigned for a moment, and the distant sounds of a fight filtered into the barn. My stomach trembled. This couldn't be happening. It shouldn't be, but it was. We'd acted too late.

Michael was here.

"Michael is leading them," Zaq confirmed. "And he's...They have him fueled up."

What did that mean? I looked over at Shem, and even in the gloom his face had drained of color. "Shem? What does that mean?"

He grabbed me by the shoulders. "It means you need to hide. You fucking hide, Rue. Do not let Michael see you, and if it looks like they're winning, you run." He turned to Zaq and Tumiel. "I need you to stay with her. Keep her safe. Get her to the church.

Save the humans if you can, but Rue must come first, do you understand?"

I grabbed his arm. "Wait. We can take them. We have reapers and Gabriel and—"

"Dammit, Rue, just do as I say," he snapped. I flinched, and his expression softened. "*Please* do as I say."

My gut was in knots as I swallowed the lump in my throat and nodded. "Okay."

His lips thinned. "No. I know that tone. You *promise* me. Give me your word right now."

Fuck. "Fine. I promise."

He gripped my chin. "No. I need a watcher's promise. No deception. No lies. Only truth."

I scanned his face, trying to read him. Why was my heart hammering? Why was there a pit of foreboding opening inside me? "Shem, what—"

"Promise me, Rue. Promise me that you'll run, hide, and survive."

I took a shuddering breath. "I promise."

He held my gaze for a long beat before finally releasing me, satisfied.

"Zaqiel?" He speared Zaq with a hard look.

"I'll keep her safe," Zaq said.

Shem cupped my face gently, then kissed me hard on the mouth, the contact brief and desperate. "Goodbye, Rue."

Gabriel locked gazes with me before following Shem and Erelim out of the door. "I'll find you. Go."

Bee grabbed my hand. "Rue, we have to go."

No. Something was wrong. Something—

"Now, Rue. We need to find Bastian."

Shit, Bastian. Panic overtook the foreboding. "Where was he last?"

"I'll find him," Zaq said. "I'll get him and the others, and we'll head for the woods."

The air fizzed with the residual power from a fight that was going on outside the barn, probably on the field in front of the house. Acres of land to battle on. Acres of open sky to clash in.

My being here made Shem vulnerable. It put our mission at risk. I had to leave him. I had to go. He'd find me. I had faith in that. "Let's go."

Tumiel made up the rear as we followed Zaq to the back of the barn, to a small door that opened onto a gravelled area where some crates were stacked. We slipped outside and crouched in the shadows.

The unmistakable sounds of battle swelled around us, but whatever was happening was occurring on the other side of the barn. We were out of sight for now, and we needed to keep it that way.

Zaq motioned for us to stay back then slipped around the barn, leaving us crouched in the darkness.

He returned a moment later. "We must keep low and run for the house." He fixed his gaze on me. "Do not look toward the fight. Do not stop. Do you understand?"

Was that fear on his face? What was happening? How many sentinels were there? Were we outnumbered. And Michael... "Zaq, what did you mean when you said Michael was fueled up?"

"Celestial power. He's brimming with it. Move now. We can talk later."

I wanted to push him for more, but there was no denying the sense of urgency that pressed in on us.

He broke away again, and this time we followed, cutting across the overgrown yard, aimed for the house several feet away.

Light flashed to our left, and the urge to look, to stop and see, was almost too much, but the pressure of Bee's hand around mine kept me focused on our destination.

A figure stepped out of the house ahead.

Bastian!

He shifted his weight from foot to foot as if it was taking all his will not to run toward us as people poured out of the door behind him and gathered in the shadow of the house.

Light flashed again, lighting up his face for a moment and highlighting the terror etched there. But his attention wasn't on me, it was on the battle raging beyond us.

His eyes grew round, mouth parting in shock.

I had to see.

I had to know.

I turned to look, and my heart stopped beating.

SHEM

I stop Gabriel outside the barn. "I need your word that if things don't go our way you'll leave. You'll find Rue and keep her safe."

"*You* need to leave," Gabriel says. "You're the only one who can put the Morningstar together. I didn't want to challenge your authority in front of Rue, but I'm doing it now."

"He's right," Erelim says. "Get back in that barn and get out of here while you can."

Their concern is touching, but... "I'm not the only one that can fix the relic."

Gabriel's eyes flare wide. "Rue..."

He'll be an asset to Rue. "Michael has no idea. Only my watchers know the truth, and now...now you two. You must keep it that way. She's the key to everything. You must keep her alive. Everything you need is at the church."

Gabriel stares at me in dawning comprehension. "No...Shem...You can't do this."

Smart, always so fucking smart. He's figured out my plan. "I have to. You'd do the same."

Erelim exhales, his silver eyes filled with sadness. "Rue will have our scythes as protection."

Gabriel's jaw hardens. "Damn you, Shemyaza. We could have been friends."

Yes. I believe we would have become fast friends with time. "In another life maybe."

Someone roars in pain, and the world is momentarily bright.

There is no more time for talk.

I launch myself into the air, wings beating hard to take me high into the sky where the battle rages.

Eight sentinels in full armor, bodies radiating celestial light, swords gleaming wickedly against the night, battle my watchers and Erelim's reapers. The sentinels may be outnumbered, but my watchers are outpowered, evidenced by the blood from their wounds that taints the air.

Erelim launches himself into the sky with a battle cry, hurtling into the midst of the fray, scythe cutting a lethal path across the stars.

But my attention is drawn to the flame that burns in the middle of the brawl.

To Michael, who shines like the sun. Light flows beneath his skin and is woven into every strand of hair on his head.

His golden armor blazes with it too.

My chest aches with longing, and tears spring to my eyes because the Dominion have indeed made him whole. But now he's also a beacon to every monster in a five-mile radius.

Rue and the humans are in danger for as long as he continues to shine here.

It's time to end his stay. "Michael!"

Michael turns in the air to face me, his gold-tipped wings flared and still, able to hold him aloft without beating.

His voice booms my name, the sound so beautiful that it makes my heart ache. I barely register the gargantuan, invisible fist that closes around my body, crushing me and holding me immobile.

"I have been charged with your execution," Michael says.

He has me in his power. There's no winning this. But then, I already knew that. I'm not here to win. Not today, anyway. My win will come later. Much later, when Rue completes the task that I couldn't.

I drop my gaze to Gabriel, still on the ground, his body tense as if torn between taking flight or running. *Go,* I mouth. *Please.*

He falters for a moment, gaze flicking from me to Michael, and then he turns and runs back into the barn.

The knot in my chest eases a little.

He'll protect her.

He'll keep her safe.

Michael hauls me toward him, his sapphire eyes blazing with zeal. His sword flashes as it comes up. I can't move. I can't defend myself.

Good.

This way I don't have to fight my primal instincts.

He can have me. Because with me gone, the Dominion will leave Rue alone. They'll think the key to fixing the Morningstar has been eliminated, and we'll have hope once more.

I'm sorry, Rue. So fucking sorry.

Fire pierces my heart, and my vision goes dark.

RUE

Shem hung suspended in the air with a sword through his chest.

Michael's sword, because Michael had stabbed him.

Stabbed him through the chest, and Shem...Shem wasn't moving.

He wasn't fucking moving.

Shards of ice exploded in my chest. "NO!"

Bee slapped her hand over my mouth, wrestling with me to stop me running toward the fight and force me into the shadows behind the house. I fought her on instinct—the need to get to Shem burning through all logic.

"Fuck!" Bee lost her grip on me, and I ran out into the moonlight.

"SHEM!" A thick arm snagged me around the waist and hauled me back. I kicked out. "No! Shem! No."

Michael's gaze locked on to me—cold fire and nothingness.

"Rue, stop!" Bastian said. "You have to fucking stop. He's gone. He's fucking gone."

"Get her!" Michael's command reverberated around me, and the next instant, every sentinel was aiming for me.

"Move!" Tumiel ordered.

Shem was dead, and if I died here, then the Dominion would win.

I stopped fighting and turned to flee, knowing deep down that it was probably too late to escape, but we ran anyway because I'd be damned if I simply rolled over and allowed myself to be executed.

My survival instinct kicked in. I'd made a promise to Shem. Hide. Run. Survive.

Barbs speared my heart and my lungs, but I kept running through the pain. There'd be time for that later if we survived.

"The woods!" Bastian yelled over and over as people, gripped with terror, scattered. "The fucking woods!" Bastian's command must have registered because people adjusted their trajectory toward the tree line and away from the open road.

We rushed across the field, a desperate horde of mortality with celestial death on our tails. Where was Gabriel? Where were the reapers and Erelim?

The sentinels closed in.

We weren't going to make it.

The shadows in the tree line shifted then burst free in the form of monsters.

Bee screamed.

But my heart leaped because I recognized the monster leading the charge as no monster at all.

"Kabiel!" His gaze swept over me in acknowledgement, then up to the sky. Wings burst from his back, and he took to the air along with the devolved watchers.

Not so devolved now.

They still had the spider legs, but they also had wings and faces, arms and hands, and Kabiel...Kabiel looked more humanoid than ever.

They attacked the sentinels, tearing a couple down from the sky and devouring them.

I caught sight of the reapers and Erelim weaving between the devolved watchers and teaming up to ward off the sentinels.

"Rue!" Gabriel joined us at the tree line just as Michael's disembodied voice filled the air.

"Fall back!" he ordered his troop. "We have what we need."

The sentinels disengaged and shot up into the air, vanishing into the night.

They were gone.

Michael was gone.

Shem was...

I fell to my knees, chest heaving as my lungs struggled against the crushing weight pressing in on them.

"Rue? Rue, get up," Bee said. "We have to go. We have to get out of here now that all the celestial light has attracted monsters."

"She's right," Kabiel said. "It's how we found you. Move. We will hold back the worst of it."

Yes, I had to move. I had to keep going, but my limbs refused to cooperate, wanting nothing but to curl into a ball.

"Find us at the church," Zaq said to Kabiel.

They were making plans. I needed to focus, but the desire to retreat into my head, into the warm fuzzy place waiting for me was too strong. For a moment, I was back at the mall in bed with Shem, playing little spoon as he cocooned me in his heat. It was safe here. Safe and warm and—

Bee slapped me hard enough to clear the fuzziness in my head. "Snap the fuck out of it. We have people to protect."

I looked up at the people around me.

My people.

My responsibility.

Gabriel and Bastian held out their hands and I reached for them, allowing them to haul me to my feet. "Stay together." My voice was a hoarse rasp. "It's going to be a long night."

CHAPTER 34

"Rue? Rue, are you listening to me?" Sarq's voice broke through the fog in my mind, and the world came sharply into focus.

The main road was to the left of the undergrowth we were trudging through to remain in the shadow of the tree line. I'd slipped from the head of the party to somewhere in the middle. I should be leading. Shem would want me to lead. To take charge. To make sure these people survived.

What was I doing? "I'm sorry. I'm okay. I'm here." I attempted to pick up the pace, but Sarq's hand fell on my shoulder, his grip firm yet gentle.

"It's all right. Gabriel and Bastian have the lead, and Erelim and Tumiel are making up the rear. Zaq is scouting, and the watchers and reapers have us flanked. We'll be fine. Another hour and we'll be there."

Another hour. How had time slipped by? Where had I gone in my head? I needed to focus. "Has Kabiel caught up to us?"

"Not yet. But I'm sure he'll find us. He knows the church."

"Good, that's...that's good."

I could feel him looking at me, studying me. Trying to figure out if I was about to fall apart. "I'll be okay, Sarq. I'm going to finish what we started. For Shem." My voice came out strong and determined, belying the quiver in my belly.

"We'll do it together," Sarq said, his voice thick with emotion. "I swear to you, Rue. I will protect you with my life." His warm, amber eyes were filled with sadness.

"I'll need a moment when we get to the church. A moment alone to...process."

He nodded. "You'll have it."

We trudged on in silence for a few minutes, and it hit me that the air of despondency came not just from inside me but from outside me too. A heavy blanket of doom loomed over us all. Of course, everyone had realized the implications of Shem's death. Realized it would affect our plan for liberation.

They thought hope was dead.

Bee joined us a moment later. "Tumiel spotted

Kabiel and the devolved watchers. They're trailing behind, keeping a distance."

"Good. That's good." My voice came out flat.

Bee slipped her hand into mine and squeezed. "Let's head up front and help scout. Zaq must be exhausted. We can give him a hand."

"I don't think that's wise," Sarq said.

"It's what we do," Bee replied. "It's what we're trained for. We'll stay close."

Sarq ignored her and looked down at me. "Will you take that risk?"

Shem was gone, and I was the only one who could put the Morningstar back together. Risks were no longer an option. I smiled at Bee. "Thanks. I know you're trying help me keep my mind active, and I appreciate it. But I'm tired. I just...I want to walk."

Her frown told me that she didn't believe me, but she nodded, accepting my excuse. I'd tell her why soon. Once we were safe. Once I had half a moment. I'd tell her what Shem's death meant and what I now needed to do.

But for everyone else, my ability needed to remain a secret just in case Michael found a way into our midst again. The less people that knew that I could fix the Morningstar, the better.

I'd have to let them believe hope was lost, at least for a while.

GABRIEL AND BASTIAN broke off their conversation as I joined them. It didn't take a genius to figure out they'd been talking about me.

"I'm fine, just to clarify. Sarq says we'll be at the church in a few minutes. It should come into view when we round the corner up ahead."

"I was saying to Gabriel that we'll need a security system," Bastian said. "I can scout for supplies once we're settled. There's a town a few miles away from the church."

"No need. The church has its own security in that no celestials or monsters come near it."

Gabriel exhaled through his nose. "So that's what Shem meant."

"What?"

"Nothing. It sounds like the church has a natural warding in place. Strange but not unheard of. Question is, who put it there?"

"No idea. But we'll be safe, and hopefully if you're with us you'll be able to see the church and get inside it."

"What about Kabiel and the devolved?" Bastian said.

"As much as I'm grateful to Kabiel, it would be

unwise to allow them inside the church with so much fleshy temptation around. I'm sure he'll agree."

"There's woodland close by," Bastian said. "I saw it on Zaq's map."

"It'll have to do. We'll get everyone settled, and first thing tomorrow I'll need to go out and scout for the relic piece."

"How will you do that?" Gabriel asked.

He was asking *how* not *why*. Had Shem told him I could fix the relic? Or was he working on the assumption that having all the pieces was still wise, that we might find another way to heal it? Either way, I trusted him, and he needed to know. "I can fix the relic, in case you were wondering why I'm still determined to find all the pieces. I can find a safe spot and open the channel for a few moments." Gabriel didn't look surprised, which meant Shem must have told him. He hadn't mentioned he knew when we'd spoken in the kitchen, but then we'd been side-tracked by my revelation that Michael might be tracking Bee. "Jilyana can help me find the pieces."

Now Gabriel looked confused. "Jilyana?"

He didn't know about her. Shem hadn't told him. "Jilyana is a djinn, and the Dominion used her to make Shem break the relic." I filled him in on Jilyana's part in all this, in her relationship with Michael and how he'd betrayed her to the Dominion and how the Dominion then used her to seduce Shem. "She got into his head and controlled him. Made him see things while she used his body to break the Morningstar. But when it fractured, a piece of it lodged inside her. That was the piece Kabiel saw in his vision."

"She was inside the Golden City?" Gabriel asked.

"Yes, and she used me to get out."

His eyes narrowed. "How can we trust her?"

"She saved my life twice. I trust her. She's at the church already. She took the children there."

He looked like he wanted to say something but was holding back.

"Spit it out, Gabriel."

"I don't think we should be so quick to let our guard down," he said. "This creature deceived Shem for her own gain once; what's to say she isn't playing another game of deception?"

"By saving my life? By healing Shem? By keeping our children safe?" Anger, sudden and unexpected gripped me. "She made a fucking mistake. One mistake by loving Michael, by trusting him with her truth, and it got her incarcerated. It put her in the bastard Dominion's clutches, and they used her. They promised her freedom and used her. She's been locked away for decades, and she deserves to be given a second chance."

"Very well," Gabriel said.

But his tone suggested otherwise. Whatever. He

could be wary if he wanted. He'd soon see that Jilyana was genuinely on our side.

We rounded the bend in the road, and the church came into view in the distance.

"Is that it?" someone cried. "We're here."

"I don't see it," Gabriel said. "There's nothing there."

The celestial power in his body was too strong, and it was blinding him to the church.

"Focus," Bastian said. "Maybe if you believe it's there?"

We crossed the road onto the stretch of overgrown land that led to the neat church with its white picket fence.

"Still nothing," Gabriel said.

I reached out and took his hand on a gut feeling. "I want you to see it." A tingle passed down my arm and through my palm.

He sucked in a breath. "What the...I see it." He looked down at my hand then back at the church. "How did you know to do that?"

I shrugged. "It felt right."

We were almost at the fence now, and all my people had picked up the pace.

"What's happening?" Erelim asked, joining us. "Where is this church?"

I touched his arm. "I want you to see it. Look."

He turned his head, and his eyes flared. "How..."

236

"Later," Gabriel said. "Get everyone inside. Rue, we need to bring the veil down for the others."

The door to the church opened, and Jilyana appeared, relief etched all over her face. Her gaze locked with mine, and she beamed before searching the crowd.

She was looking for Shem.

My heart sank, and I turned away. Breaking the news to her would have to wait a few moments. I had reapers whose eyes needed to be opened and beyond that, in the shadows, lurked Kabiel and the devolved. I needed to speak to them too.

"I'll tell her," Bastian said. "You sort the reapers and speak to Kabiel."

I loved how he was on the same wavelength as me.

He kissed my forehead and broke away, heading to the gate and the church, where Jilyana waited with her hand on her chest.

She knew.

She already knew.

BEE INSISTED on coming with me to speak to Kabiel while everyone else went into the church.

The devolved watchers were hidden in the forest on the other side of the road across from the church, but Kabiel stood in the moonlight waiting for us. He looked taller out here in the open—over seven feet off the ground, his body held aloft by his spider legs. He lowered himself as I approached, legs contracting like pistons. The usual shudder that went through me at the sight of his arachnid form was absent. Numbed by everything that had happened.

Bee grabbed my hand to stall me.

"It's okay. Kabiel won't hurt me."

She looked wary but released me and trailed behind as I bridged the distance between me and the watcher.

His shadow fell over me, and he crouched further, tucking in his chin to look down at me. "It's been a long time since I was here."

"You'll stay in the woods for now. I know you guys are fueled up with celestial power, but aside from the fact that it'll be cramped inside, I don't think it's a good idea for you to be so close to people."

His mouth twisted in a wry smile. "I agree. But you need not worry. We cannot enter. We can barely approach. The church wards off monsters. And even with the gift you have given us, we are still more monster than watcher."

So the celestials were blind to this place and monsters could see it but not approach it.

"Why is this place special?" Bee asked.

Kabiel turned his attention to her. "We do not

know, and although we attempted to understand it, we failed to do so. Maybe you will discover something we missed."

I didn't have time for this. "I don't care about the damn church and its mystery. As long as it keeps my people safe, it can keep its secrets."

Kabiel let out a ragged sigh. "You're in pain. Angry. I'm sorry we were too late in finding you."

The hollow pit inside me yawned wider, threatening to swallow me. I exhaled and looked away, not wanting to see the sympathy in his eyes.

"I doubt there was much you could have done," Bee said. "Michael came with a mission. The Dominion powered him up for it. I doubt anyone could have stopped him."

"A great light was extinguished today," Kabiel said softly. "Its absence will be felt for eternity."

My throat pinched painfully as I forced myself to look at him again. "We'll finish what he started. I'm going to try to get a lock on the relic starting tomorrow."

"Ah...there is hope yet, then?" He searched my face, and I nodded. "I suspected you may be the key. I see he realized it too. I suppose it gave him comfort to know that he wasn't the only one who could save us."

Shem was gone but hearing him referred to in the past tense hurt. "Can you stop...Stop talking about him in the past tense."

Compassion rippled across his alien features. "He *is* gone, and you must accept it. Grieve if you must and then move on. You cannot afford to be hindered by sorrow. It was why Shem kept himself apart. Why he shielded his heart. He knew that attachments could weaken him at the most inopportune time. That he couldn't let anything hold him back from achieving his goal. That responsibility now falls to you."

But Shem had let his guard down for me. He'd loved me, and now he was dead. Would he be alive if he hadn't given his heart to me? Would he have made different choices, choices that would have kept him out of Michael's grasp?

Had I weakened him? Had I caused his death?

My eyes burned as a fist closed around my heart.

"You're wrong," Bee snapped. "Love makes us stronger. It helps us to fight harder."

A few of the devolved chittered in agitation, and Bee flinched but held her ground.

Kabiel hissed, and they shut up. "Love also impairs judgment. It skews priorities."

I didn't have the emotional or mental energy for this. "None of that matters now, though, does it? Shem is gone. He's fucking gone, and we have to carry on. We have to make his death mean something. And you... you need to have a fucking vision."

"I don't control the visions, Rue. They come to me when the time is right. You must have faith."

"Faith? Is there any point when no one is listening? No. I'm not leaving things to chance." I grabbed his face and opened the door to the Morningstar power.

It hit him in a jet of power. He cried out, eyes glowing bright silver for a moment.

Chitters rose in the air behind him.

"Rue, stop!" Bee demanded. "Stop now."

I cut off the power and dropped my hands. "There you go. That should increase the odds of a vision, right?" My tone was bitter. My soul was bitter. And for a moment, I hated the world. Hated that I had to be here without Shem. That this world had to matter more to me than he did. "Find me if you see anything."

I strode off toward the church, and Bee hurried to catch up.

"How will he find you? He can't get close to the church," Bee said.

"He doesn't need to. If Kabiel wants to speak to me, he can walk into my dreams."

I pushed open the gate and headed up the path toward the church. The door opened, and Jilyana stood on the doorstep, her eyes glittering with tears.

No. I couldn't deal with her right now. I didn't want to deal with anyone.

I brushed past her, down the aisle, avoiding looking at anyone as I beelined for the room at the back that Shem and I had first...

No.

Keep it together.

I closed and locked the door, and when I turned to face the room, my gaze zeroed in on the spot where Shem and I had first consummated our relationship.

He'd kissed me for the first time in this space.

A bubble of emotion swelled inside me as my heart beat hard and heavy. My knees went weak, and I slid to the floor, surrendering to the pain.

Shem was gone. I'd never get to touch him, hold him, see his wicked smile or breathe in his scent. He was gone, and I'd never get to hear his rumbling voice or his rare laughter. Our last moments together filled my mind.

The torment in his eyes just before he'd kissed me and said goodbye.

Goodbye...He'd said *goodbye*. As if he'd known he wasn't coming back.

Needles of ice pricked at my scalp.

Had he known?

CHAPTER 35

BASTIAN

Rue's sobs filter through the thick wooden door, and it takes every ounce of my willpower not to hammer on it and ask her to let me in. But she needs this moment alone, and I have to respect that, no matter how impotent it makes me feel.

Bee joins me at the door. "She's gonna be okay. We just need to give her time and support."

"I know, I just...I was banking on Shem being here to pick up the pieces when *I'm* gone, and now...Fuck. I can't do this to her again."

Bee squeezes my arm. "Rue's strong, and there's time to save you. I know we can."

I want to believe that, but my gut tells me different. My body is shot, and I'm hanging on by a thread, but now with Shem gone I need to fight harder. I won't leave her yet. I can't. She needs me.

"We should go back into the main room. Give her some space," Bee says. "Right now, these people need a leader, and with Shem gone, they'll be looking to Rue and the watchers. They don't know Gabriel or Erelim." Her mouth lifted in half a smile. "Even though Gabriel is doing his best to organize everyone right now."

"What about Tumiel and the others?"

"They've, uh...they've retreated."

"They're grieving too. They just lost their leader."

"We should help." She looks back at the door, clearly as torn as I am. I mean, she came here for the same reason as me—to check on Rue. All we are doing is trying to talk ourselves out of taking the action that we want to take.

Rue's sobs have died down, and I imagine her in the room alone, bereft and heartbroken. "Fuck it. If she wants us gone, she'll tell us to fuck off."

Bee lifts her chin. "Do it."

I knock. "Rue? Rue, it's Bastian."

"And Bee."

Silence greets us.

I rest my forehead to the wood. "Rue, we just...We want to be with you through this."

"Please open the door," Bee adds.

A soft click, and the door swings open to reveal

Rue, red-eyed and puffy-faced. Her mouth trembles, and her eyes well up.

Bee and I cross the threshold, and she steps into our arms.

GABRIEL

Rue's pain, acute and sharp, cuts into me over and over. The shield that I've put up between us feels flimsy. I'll need to work on strengthening it, otherwise I'll be encroaching on her privacy.

The bond created between us through the choosing is stronger than expected. Probably because a piece of Shem's soul lives inside of her, the part that is most connected to the Morningstar. Whatever it is, I feel her, and if not for the shield that I've erected, she'd feel me too.

The church has several rooms, and the human Mira is attempting to organize everyone, but arguments have broken out over who should take which spot because this is meant to be their permanent home now, and as far as they're aware, all hope of saving this world died with Shem.

The mood is low. Anger and despondency taint the air. These people are exhausted, both physically and mentally, and if someone doesn't step into Shem's shoes, then this small community will fall apart.

But Shem's watchers have retreated onto the upper floor, and Baraqel and his scouts are nowhere to be seen. I'm certain that Shem's troop knows of Rue's ability, but I doubt that the rest of the watchers do. They probably think that hope is dead.

"It'll be chaos without direction," Erelim says. "Should we step in?"

I didn't come here to lead. It was never my forte, and these people don't know me, but I can support the true leader. The person these people should look up to.

Rue.

"It's not our place to lead here, Erelim, but we can help Rue and Shem's watchers. These people know her. They understand her importance and her connection to the Morningstar."

"Maybe they should know that all hope is not lost," Erelim says. "That we can still fix their world. This place is a sanctuary and they're safe here. There is no way for the Dominion to discover the truth."

He's right, and I'd agree to reveal it to them except...My gaze falls on Jilyana standing by the alter area past the crossing section of the church. Her eyes are dull and red-rimmed from crying at the news of Shem's death. But how real is her grief?

This creature deceived two celestials.

She fractured this world.

"I don't trust the djinn."

Erelim follows my gaze. "Ah...yes...I see."

"Until we can be sure of her motives, the truth about Rue's ability must remain a secret held by a trusted few."

"And Rue? Does she trust the djinn?"

"Yes."

"In that case, you'll need to speak to her and convince her not to confide in the djinn."

"No, I told you already!" Mira's voice rises in exasperation as people close in around her. There's panic in her eyes as she scans the room, as if searching for a lifeline.

Fuck it. "Enough!"

My voice is a boom that reverberates around the chamber, and all eyes turn to me: inquisitive, frowning, upset.

I don't give a shit. "Shemyaza died so that all of you could be safe, and this is how you repay him? By bickering over inconsequential things such as rooms? Be grateful you have a roof to shelter under. Be grateful that you have your lives."

Several people drop their heads in shame.

"But for how long?" someone demands. "Shemyaza is dead, which means we're fucked. Who's going to fix the Morningstar and get us our world back?"

"I don't know." I lift my chin. "But what I do know is that if you fight amongst yourselves, none of you will live to find out the answer." I step forward into the crowd. "While there is life, there is hope. Believe that we will find another way. Trust in that." I look to Mira. "Allocate whatever rooms you see fit, and if anyone argues, they can sleep on the pews."

Mira nods curtly. "You heard him. Now listen up..."

I walk away, and Erelim follows, leaving her in charge once more.

"We should speak to the watchers," Erelim says. "Tell them what we've learned of the Dominion's plans and tell them about the human resistance."

"Yes, but not without Rue." I glance across the room, toward the door that leads to the back of the church. "Not tonight. Tonight everyone needs a moment to breathe and process. Tomorrow we'll make plans."

CHAPTER 36

RUE

Bastian and Bee left me to get myself cleaned up in the small washroom off the study. I was grateful for their comfort, but I needed a moment to collect myself. Alone.

My head was fuzzy from crying, and although the awful weight of loss that sat on my chest was still there, a part of me felt lighter. I'd have to learn to live with these feelings. This emptiness. Learn to accept it as a part of me.

But for now, I needed to pull my shit together.

I had people to organize, and I needed to knock heads with the watchers, Gabriel, and the reapers to formulate a plan.

The woman who looked back at me from the bathroom mirror was pale and haggard looking. This wasn't the face of a leader. Not the face of authority my people needed.

I splashed cold water on my face and patted it dry with my sleeve. Better. Okay.

I made it to the foot of the narrow staircase that led to the upper floor—one of three staircases in the church —when the sound of voices had me slowing my pace.

"Did you see Michael's power? The Dominion gave him that. They gifted it to him, and he was whole. We should have never listened to Shem. We should have thrown ourselves on the mercy of the Golden City."

I recognized the nasal pitched voice of one of Baraqel's scouts, Menuqel.

"There's still time," another scout named Cariel said. "Baraqel wanted this, and Shem convinced him otherwise. We can do it now. We can go."

"We have no bargaining chip."

"We have the humans. They want humans," Cariel said.

"I don't know…"

"Do you want to devolve? Because with Shem gone, that's what will happen."

I could have stepped out and corrected them. Told them that there was hope. But these bastards didn't deserve that.

No. I knew exactly what they deserved.

THE CHURCH WAS a three-story affair with several rooms on each floor and three bathrooms. Once my people settled in their rooms, and the main chamber with the pews was free, I called a meeting with the watchers and the reapers. Jilyana and Bee sat at the back of the room with Bastian.

"Rue, can I have a word quickly?" Gabriel asked.

I wanted to get on with my plan, but he looked like he had something important on his mind. "Sure." We stepped to one side, away from the main group. "What's up?"

"I don't think you should make your ability common knowledge."

"My ability?"

He exhaled and leaned in to whisper. "That you can fix the relic."

I didn't plan to make it common knowledge, especially after what I'd just overheard, but I needed to know why he didn't want me to spill the beans. "Why not?"

"Because I'm not sure you can trust everyone here. Especially not the djinn."

"Jilyana saved my life."

"I know, and I might be wrong, but I strongly

advise that we err on the side of caution. Give it a few days at least. Wait. It's what Shem would want."

Anger ignited in my chest. "How the fuck do you know what Shem would want in this situation? It's not like he knew that he was going to…" Oh…My earlier suspicion surged to the forefront of my mind as his expression clouded. "He knew…"

"Yes. I didn't want to tell you like this. I was hoping to speak to you tomorrow after you'd rested, but…Yes, he knew. He knew they'd keep chasing him, so he gave himself to them to end their pursuit. He sacrificed himself so that the Dominion would leave you alone."

The barbed ball of emotion inside me swelled, pricking at my senses and bringing tears to my eyes. No. Not here. Not now.

"He asked me to look out for you," Gabriel said.

"You let him do it? You let him die?" My eyes burned with rage as I settled my gaze on Gabriel. "Why didn't you stop him?" My voice was a strangled whisper when all I wanted to do was scream.

"Because I knew he wouldn't have let me, and because…because I knew it was the right call."

I wanted to punch him in his beautiful face. I wanted to scream and cry, but these were the emotions of the human who Shem had found on the road. The woman who I'd become while in his company knew better. She understood why he'd made this sacrifice, even though it tore her up inside. She understood it because she would have done the same.

I swallowed against the bitterness in my throat. "Thank you for telling me."

"Will you respect his wishes and mine? Wait a while before telling everyone?"

If I waited, then I could weed out all the people that might turn against us. Jilyana could stay in the dark a little longer. "I'll wait. But Bee and Bastian are in the circle of trust."

He nodded. "So this meeting? Do you still need it?"

He thought I'd called the meeting to tell everyone that I could fix the Morningstar. My lips curled in a thin smile. "This meeting is about clearing out the trash." I indicated one of the pews pushed against the wall. "Take a pew."

I returned to the group, now engaged in conversations of their own.

Sarq walked over to join me at the front of the room, and after a moment, Tumiel and Zaq followed. They flanked me, arms crossed, silent and waiting, lending me support for whatever I had to say.

I should have spoken to them first, I guessed. Touched base and grieved alongside them. They were my family, and I shouldn't have retreated from them. But there'd be time to connect with them later.

Right now, I had some rats to dispose of.

"What is this about?" Baraqel demanded from his spot by one of the stained-glass windows.

"Setting a few ground rules."

"And who put you in charge?"

"You will, I hope."

His eyebrows went up, and he let out a bark of laughter. "Shemyaza is gone. Our hope is gone, and you...you no longer matter."

"Do you truly believe that?"

His eyes narrowed.

"Or is that grief speaking? Because grief I can accept, but dissention and traitorous thoughts, I will not." My tone was cold. "Shem might be gone, but we're still here. All of us—humans, watchers, and celestials. We're still here, and so there's hope. I still have a connection to the Morningstar, and I *will* find a way to fix things. It might take longer, but I vow to you, I'll make it happen. So the question is, who's with me?"

"We are," Sarq said, speaking for Shem's troop.

"You have my reapers," Erelim added.

"And me," Gabriel added. "For what it's worth."

"We're with you," Penemue and Amaros said.

But my focus was on Baraqel. He was the one I needed on board. The one who controlled the scouts who made up the bulk of our watchers.

He locked gazes with me. "Shem and I may not have seen eye to eye, but I respected him. He was...a friend. I made a vow to him a long time ago to protect humanity, to find a cure for the sickness that he unwittingly created." He shot a glare in Jilyana's direction. "I will not turn from that vow now. You have me and my scouts."

The knot in my chest eased a little, but not all the way because there was still one more step. "And do you have your scouts under control, Baraqel?"

His eyes narrowed. "You insult me with that question."

"It's not my intention to insult you. I need to know what you would do to a scout that betrayed you. To a scout that voices traitorous thoughts at this delicate time. What would you do to a scout that considered giving the humans to the Dominion to save their own skin?" I looked right at Menuqel and Cariel as I said the words, and their faces drained of color. "What would you do then, Baraqel?"

Baraqel followed my gaze, comprehension dawning across his terrifying features. "What did you do?" he demanded of the pair.

"Nothing," Menuqel said. "We haven't done anything yet."

"But we should," Cariel replied, defiance etched across his face. "The Dominion made Michael whole, and if we give them the humans, then they can—" Baraqel's hand whipped out, talons slashing across Cariel's throat.

Blood spurted, and the watcher hit the ground on

his knees, hands going up to try and cover the wound, while he stared up at Baraqel in shock. But his eyes quickly drifted closed, and he fell onto his side, dead.

Menuqel stepped back, hands going up to ward off Baraqel. "Please. I'm sorry. I'm—"

Baraqel jerked his head toward his other scouts, who grabbed hold of Menuqel.

"You wanted to make a deal with the Dominion at one time," Menuqel said. "You were going to betray Shem."

Baraqel's jaw hardened, his lip curling in disgust. "Back then, we didn't know the truth of what they do to the humans in their care. We didn't know that they'd orchestrated this mess. Back then, I was a blind fool, but what is your excuse?"

He didn't wait for an answer before snapping the watcher's neck.

He turned to me, chest heaving with emotion. "You have my support, human." He strode from the room and out into the night.

I let him go. He'd done exactly what I'd hoped.

The rats were gone, and the standard had been set.

Traitors would meet death.

No trial.

No jury.

And going forward, that would be my way.

CHAPTER 37

Bee helped me clear out the study and turn it into a sleep area. There was bedding and supplies in the basement of the church. The watchers had always kept this place as a potential hideout. Like Shem had said, it was only the distance that needed to be traveled to get here that had kept them from using this place. They hadn't wanted to risk losing any of the humans.

We set out mattresses and blankets on the floor. This room would be a nest for me and my watchers. Bee and Bastian would sleep in here too, and Mira if she wanted. The watchers needed to be close to me to feed off the residual power of the Morningstar.

I cleaned and adjusted until my limbs ached and my eyes were heavy.

"Hey." Bastian gently cupped my shoulders. "We should sleep."

I looked about the room to find it already filled with the watchers. When had they come in?

Tumiel and Bee had taken a bed, and Zaq and Mira another. Sarq stood by the door looking uncomfortable. I held out my hand to him. "You can sleep beside me and Bastian."

Our bed was in the center of the nest to allow the watchers to have contact with me during the night. They'd reach out to touch my hand or foot or stroke my hair, reacting to the Morningstar power that resonated through me.

"I'll be sleeping in the scouts' room tomorrow."

Bastian tensed. "What?"

"I won't allow them to devolve." The watchers were connected to the Morningstar power through Shem, and his troop had been the closest to that power. It was how so many watchers had resisted devolution all this time. But now...now, I was the only connection to the Morningstar. They needed me, and if we were going to fix this world, then I needed them. "With Shem...with him gone, the connection to the power is weaker for our group. I need to keep all our active watchers fueled."

"I'll speak to Baraqel tomorrow," Tumiel said. "We'll figure out a rota so that every watcher benefits."

I settled onto the mattress with Bastian playing big

spoon, and Sarq lay facing me, his amber eyes gleaming dully in the gloom.

"It will be all right," he said softly. "We will finish what Shem started. I vow it."

My smile felt out of place on my face, at odds with the sadness inside me. "Thank you."

"Sleep now," Bastian said. "We've got you."

COOL MARBLE KISSED the bare soles of my feet, and warm air brushed across my cheeks. When I opened my eyes, I was in a moonlit room with a high ceiling and vaulted windows on either side of me.

The room was bare, and there were no doors that I could see. Curiosity tugged me toward one of the windows that depicted a blanket of stars. I was high up, so high that the strange world below looked like a carefully crafted model. The distant red skies seemed fake, and the mountains peaked with flame looked like part of the model landscape. Gray and frosty in one place and an inferno of reds and oranges in another.

What was this?

I was dreaming.

This was a dream.

The air behind me shifted, and I turned to find a woman standing in the center of the room. She was tall, at least six feet, built like a warrior, her inky dark hair coiled on her head adding another few inches to her height, and her pale eyes were hard chips of ice as they raked me over. She was dressed in leather armor which was speckled with dark patches. Blood maybe? There were a few spots of it on her face also.

She rasied her chin. "About time. Although you're not what I expected. A mortal with the seed of a celestial soul? *He* is getting inventive in His old age, it seems."

He? My scalp prickled. "Who are you?"

She snorted indelicately. "Has the journey here addled your mind?"

She waved her hand, and a table appeared, housing a goblet. She picked it up and took a long gulp of the contents. "Infernal Skitteraptors." She rolled her shoulders. "Nasty beasts." She took another sip.

"This is a dream. I need to wake up."

She peered at me over the rim of the goblet, eyes narrowing slightly. "You're not physically here. You're astral." She exhaled, clearly annoyed. "I don't have time for this. He either wants me to rise, or He doesn't. Tell Him to stop playing games. I've done my part. I've watched over His fucking zoo for long enough. I want out."

If my confusion showed on my face, she didn't notice. "I don't understand."

She stared at me as if I was a moron and then frowned. "He did send you, didn't He?"

"I have no idea what you're talking about."

She rolled her eyes. "God. Did He send you or not?"

"What? No. I...I don't know how I got here. I was sleeping and...Who are you? What is this place?"

She set the goblet down, her gaze suddenly intense and probing. "My name is Lucifer, and this is Gehenna, and if you're here but He *didn't* send you, then something has gone terribly wrong."

CHAPTER 38

DOMINION

Shemyaza's wounds heal, but we are not surprised. He was created specifically by God to guard the Morningstar; we suspected he may not be so easily destroyed. He is connected to the relic, and maybe its continued existence is what keeps him alive, or maybe the fact that a fraction of his soul thrives elsewhere is what prevents us from ending him. We could order the human found and exterminated to test our theory, but she is more use to us alive. Free. Believing that she is a master of her own destiny, just as Michael believes himself to be.

Our plan is working perfectly, and soon all the pieces will be in place.

Shemyaza lives on.

But we will ensure he never wakes.

Rue's adventure concludes in When Monsters Fight. *Grab your copy now!*

OTHER BOOKS BY DEBBIE CASSIDY

You can find a list of Debbie's books on her website
debbiecassidyauthor.com or on her Amazon Author Page.

There are so many worlds to choose from.

Happy reading.

About the Author

Debbie Cassidy lives in England, Bedfordshire, with her three kids and very supportive husband. Coffee and chocolate biscuits are her writing fuels of choice, and she is still working on getting that perfect tower of solitude built in her back garden. Obsessed with building new worlds and reading about them, she spends her spare time daydreaming and conversing with the characters in her head—in a totally non-psychotic way, of course. She writes Urban Fantasy Romance, Paranormal Reverse Harem Romance, and Sci Fi Romance.

STAY IN TOUCH WITH DEBBIE CASSIDY

Join her <u>Newsletter</u>

Hang out in her <u>Facebook Reader Group</u>

or

Follow her on <u>Bookbub</u>

Printed in Great Britain
by Amazon

39301974R00158